"Miss. . . ? You don't look well. You should rest."

"W–w–wa–ter. . . ," she whispered, her voice as hoarse as sandpaper.

As though his touch robbed her strength, she folded, her eyes fluttering back in her head as they closed.

"Miss!"

Clay caught her in his arms before she hit dirt and lowered himself to the ground, holding her. Helpless, he looked around, hoping to find an answer in the empty valley. No one or nothing else explained her presence. It was as if she'd appeared out of the shimmering air, though of course that was impossible. Likely she'd emerged from beyond one of the nearby bluffs where he hadn't been looking; they contained enough hollows and jagged edges to conceal a person.

She felt solid and warm, her body trembling against him—nothing ghostlike about her. Clay then noticed her hands, and his stomach clenched in horrified pity.

Black soot covered them, and serious burns had eaten away at her palms and fingers, leaving angry red blisters. He doubted she would ever regain good use of her hands. If she lived at all.

PAMELA GRIFFIN lives in Texas and divides her time among family, church activities, and writing. She fully gave her life to the Lord in 1988 after a rebellious young adulthood and owes the fact that she's still alive today to an all-loving, forgiving God and a mother who prayed that her wayward daughter would come "home." Pamela's main goal in writing Christian romance is to encourage others through entertaining stories that also heal the wounded spirit. Please visit Pamela at: www.Pamela-Griffin.com.

Books by Pamela Griffin

HEARTSONG PRESENTS

Don't miss out on any of our super romances. Write to us at the following address for information on our newest releases and club information.

Heartsong Presents Readers' Service
PO Box 721
Uhrichsville, OH 44683

Or visit www.heartsongpresents.com

A Treasure Revealed

Pamela Griffin

Heartsong Presents

With much gratitude to my dear friends who've been there for me in a pinch: Theo, Therese, Paige, Jill, and my mother, always there to help when my deadline lurks ever closer.

Involvement in daily life sometimes shields the treasures right before us, and we tend to look beyond; to try to find what we think will make us happy. So at this time, I want to thank You, Lord, for my many treasures: my two sons, more precious to me than gold or silver; my priceless family and friends; and above all, You, God, and the invaluable love You have always shown me. Thank You for this journey that we've taken together.

A note from the Author:
I love to hear from my readers! You may correspond with me by writing:

Pamela Griffin
Author Relations
PO Box 721
Uhrichsville, OH 44683

ISBN 978-1-60260-286-1

A TREASURE REVEALED

All scripture quotations are taken from the King James Version of the Bible.

Our mission is to publish and distribute inspirational products offering exceptional value and biblical encouragement to the masses.

PRINTED IN THE U.S.A.

one

Silverton, Nevada
1869

After all Clayton Burke had endured, the possibility of a scorpion sting or a sidewinder's strike wouldn't be half as painful as working with his scoundrel brother to locate their pa's silver mine. Bad enough Derek should find a treasure like Penny for a wife. Seemed an unjust reward for absconding with Clay's portion of the map and their half sister's in what had been Pa's only legacy to his offspring.

But then, life had never been fair.

Life hadn't been fair to lure their pa away to abandon his family in his lust for wealth. It hadn't been fair to flee from their ma and allow death to steal her before her time. And life sure wasn't fair to force Clay and Derek back together in what must be the biggest mistake ever recorded.

Clay didn't trust Derek's sudden change of heart, didn't trust anything about the man he hadn't seen in over four years—ever since he'd ambled into town to visit their ma's gravesite, boss Clay around and make living arrangements for him, then amble back out the following day.

Frowning, Clay rode southwest through scrub and brush, over high desert and barren valley in what his map portion revealed as the direction to the silver. At least his section contained the *X*. He figured the treasure shouldn't be difficult to find, being as the only river running east to west that he'd heard of in these parts was the Humboldt. Both river and

5

location covered his portion of map, and though he wasn't sure of the distance, he should be able to find the mine without the other two-thirds to guide him. He hadn't resorted to thievery to aid his goal. Unlike his snake of a brother, Derek.

Steam rose off Clay's damp clothes, the cloudburst of earlier chased away by the sun that again blazed its habitual scorching rays. The rain shower—brief though it had been—had surprised Clay. From what little he'd experienced of this part of the West, the land didn't receive its fair portion of cooling water from above. He supposed even nature played unfair. Or maybe it was God who doled out the elements unjustly. Clay winced. Had his ma been alive and able to hear his irreverent thoughts, she might have pulled him by his ear out to the woodshed, regardless that he'd just passed his twentieth year. He turned his attention to the south, then north. Only mile after mile of confounded rock and scrub and bluff. She'd have a hard time finding a tree, let alone a woodshed.

No sooner had the thought crossed his mind than what must have been a mirage materialized in the shimmering heat above the dirt again baked dry.

"What the. . .that's impossible."

Mystified by what he thought he saw, he rubbed bleary eyes, sure his inability to sleep the night before played tricks on his mind, with the intolerable heat as an ally. He brought his horse around and rode closer, but the mirage didn't evaporate into the wavering air.

"Incredible." He kicked his heels into the horse's sides and took off at a pounding gallop toward a young woman staggering in his direction at least fifty feet ahead.

"Miss, are you all right?" he called out as he brought his horse to a swift halt near her and realized she was far from being well. Her straggled hair hung well below her shoulders, her blouse and skirt were torn, and a mix of black soot and dried mud covered her from head to toe. A vacant look swam in her tawny eyes, made even more startling by the smoke-black smudges that rimmed them.

His sudden appearance didn't alarm her; she continued staring straight ahead, with no acknowledgement that she noticed him. Prickles raced along his spine at her unnatural behavior, as though he weren't visible, and the most unsettling notion slipped through his mind that *she* was the ghost.

Both to rid himself of the absurd idea and to give her needed support, he dismounted and caught up to where she stumbled. He reached out to grasp her elbow. "Miss. . . ? You don't look well. You should rest."

"W–w–wa–ter. . . ," she whispered, her voice as hoarse as sandpaper.

As though his touch robbed her strength, she folded, her eyes fluttering back in her head as they closed.

"Miss!"

Clay caught her in his arms before she hit dirt and lowered himself to the ground, holding her. Helpless, he looked around, hoping to find an answer in the empty valley. No one or nothing else explained her presence. It was as if she'd appeared out of the shimmering air, though of course that was impossible. Likely she'd emerged from beyond one of the nearby bluffs where he hadn't been looking; they contained enough hollows and jagged edges to conceal a person.

She felt solid and warm, her body trembling against him—nothing ghostlike about her. Clay then noticed her hands, and his stomach clenched in horrified pity.

Black soot covered them, and serious burns had eaten away at her palms and fingers, leaving angry red blisters. He doubted she would ever regain good use of her hands. If she lived at all.

Ripping the knot from the rain-dampened kerchief around his throat, he gently patted her hands with it. She moaned but otherwise didn't stir. He dribbled more water over her hands from the canteen at his hip then put it to her lips. She didn't swallow or choke. The precious water streamed from her slack lips into her hair. She lay as one asleep, a tattered rag doll.

At a loss and desperate for direction, Clay held the pitiful creature, her head in his lap, and begged her to wake up. He stroked the ash-coated hair at her scalp. His fingers came in contact with a nasty lump on the side of her head, and he realized the groan he heard came from his own throat.

He should find her family. Surely they were close. As gently as he could, Clay tied the wet bandanna around her hands then lifted the poor woman onto his saddle and swung up behind her. Holding her slight body tight against him, he urged his horse forward. After scouting the area, he realized that he and the woman were the only two souls in the entire valley—and if he didn't find the help she needed soon, he might be the only one left alive. He gave up looking for her kin and guided his horse in the direction he'd come as fast as he dared go in the heat so as not to kill the horse. His sister-in-law could help with her box of herbs and cure-alls. Silverton lay several hours southeast. With luck on his side, he could get there by nightfall.

The last thing Clay desired was to return to the hotel and face the rogue who called himself brother, but he wouldn't risk a woman's life due to years of ill feeling between himself and Derek.

Halfway to Silverton, he heard her groan and knew relief. She'd been so still and silent he'd been half afraid he was too late. He slowed his horse to a walk, bending close to speak with her.

"Miss?"

Her blackened eyelids didn't flicker, and he wondered if he'd imagined her moan. If not for the slim thread of erratic thumps from her heart against his arm he'd think her already dead. An odd surge of protective emotion rose from his belly, choking his throat, and his eyes misted for the frail, broken stranger who rested against him, so childlike and helpless in his arms.

A prayer rose to his lips, from what source he didn't know but imagined it was owing to his ma, who'd raised him to fear the Almighty. He held little hope of his prayer being answered but muttered it anyhow. "Please, God. Don't let her die."

At fifteen, he'd watched his ma take her final breath, the sight horrifying to behold. A light of peace had entered her eyes before she closed them for the last time, but not before Clay witnessed her misery for days on end, her wasted body writhing, agonized moans ripping through her croaky throat as she cried out for both her sons. Only Clay had been there, and it hadn't been enough. It had never been enough.

He couldn't—wouldn't—be a helpless onlooker to another pointless death, this time to a woman so young she had yet to live.

After what seemed an eternity, Silverton appeared on the horizon, the mountains beyond. The small mining town stood washed in a silver glow as a full moon rose beyond canvas tents of establishments clustered along the town's one street. He heard the warbling of a harmonica before he spotted Livvie sitting on a barrel outside the hotel. Thinking it odd his sister-in-law hadn't ordered her daughter to bed by such a late hour, Clay started to call out, when Livvie spotted him. Her mouth dropped open, the moonlight making the whites of her eyes glow as they grew even bigger.

"Uncle Clay?"

"Go fetch your mama. Tell her to bring her remedy box, then ask Shorty to tend my horse."

As though she'd lost her ability to hear, Penny's girl continued to stare at the woman who lay like one dead against him.

"Hurry, Livvie!"

"Yes, sir!" She shot up from the ground and raced inside, dark braids bouncing against her back.

It was no easy task, dismounting while taking care that the woman didn't plummet to the ground, but Clay managed. He tugged her arm, allowing her to fall into both of his, and turned toward the entrance, the woman held tight against his chest, her head hanging slack over his arm. She appeared so broken, and Clay sensed her body wasn't all that had been wounded.

Penny raced outside with her remedy box. She hesitated in clear shock before continuing his way. "Whatever has happened?"

"I found her wandering in the wilderness as if she hadn't a lick of sense. She keeled over before she could tell me anything."

Penny blinked up at Clay as if her mind was a blank.

"Penny?" he urged.

She shook off whatever ailed her and took charge. "Take her to the cubicle Mr. Matthis gave. 'Tis private. Olivia, tell Linda I'm in need of her help, then go and ready yourself for bed like you should have done. We'll sleep in the wagon tonight."

"Mama!" Livvie complained.

"Now then, I'll be hearin' no more of your impertinence." Her words were both soft and stern as she pressed the back of her hand against the woman's forehead to check for fever. She had yet to see her hands still bound in the bandanna Clay had kept damp throughout their ride.

Livvie kicked at the dirt. "Aw, just when things was gettin' exciting." She disappeared into the hotel at the same time

Derek's tall form emerged. Livvie offered him a hug in passing, and he laid his hand against the back of her head. The brief contact made Clay's insides churn. His excuse for a brother didn't deserve a family, least of all a loving one.

Clay clenched his teeth, redirecting his attention to Penny. "Did I hear you say Linda's back?"

"Aye. She arrived a little over an hour ago. Tonight must be a night for homecomings."

Relieved his half sister hadn't become a victim of the harsh land or the miners who'd claimed it, Clay opened his mouth to retort that he had no intention of remaining in Silverton any longer than necessary. Once he felt assured the desert waif he held in his arms would live, he planned to resume his journey in search of the mine. Before he could say so, Penny turned and hurried inside, first whispering to Derek, who nodded and moved away. Clay followed Penny, deciding further conversation should wait.

His sister-in-law guided him to the same room Linda had once used. Penny pulled back the muslin weighted by stones, and Clay walked ahead of her into the small cubicle, noticing Christa asleep on the ground in one corner. With care, he laid the inert woman on the largest of the thick hides. Silverton's hotel hardly deserved so fine a name, but at least it provided shelter from the elements, and Jinx, the cook, often rustled up a good meal to fill a man's belly. Even a hovel like this was preferable for the injured woman; thick canvas walls and roof helped shield from the hot days of unrelenting sun that baked a person dry and kept out the chills at night that were sometimes so cold he felt as if his very bones were shaking inside his skin.

The young woman trembled, and he wondered if it was due to the cold. He reached for another hide to cover her.

"No, Clay." Penny stopped him. "You must leave while I see to her. Would you mind taking Christa?"

"Right." Gently, he scooped up his sleeping niece, who nestled her head closer against his shoulder like a contented kitten. She yawned, her downy lashes slitting open. "Uncle Clay." She gave him a drowsy smile and closed her eyes, her small arm sliding around his neck. Before he could beat a hasty retreat and give Penny the privacy needed, he remembered his cursory examination of the woman. "Her hands. Check her hands first."

He pulled aside the muslin covering the door, his attention on Penny, and almost ran smack into Linda coming inside.

"Oh!" The redhead clasped a hand to her heart. "Clay. . ."

"Linda." He hoped his uneasy grin and gentle utterance of her name told her what he didn't have time to say.

She nodded with a smile, as if to assure him she understood his unspoken sentiment—that he'd never meant her harm and felt relieved to see her well. Added to that, the hundred and one other things he wished to discuss with his half sister.

Her eyes drifted down to the bundle Clay held, and a wistful smile touched her lips. "She's precious. So tiny, like a little doll."

Clay would have liked to talk further, but the little doll was beginning to fidget, and Clay didn't think Penny would be too happy if they woke her with their conversation. From his short experience as an uncle, he knew how hard it was getting Christa back to sleep.

"I need to take her out to the wagon."

"Of course."

Clay left the hotel and strode to the spot where Derek kept the conveyance. Being careful not to wake her, he laid Christa on a blanket Penny kept on the floorboards. The tarpaulin remained intact, shielding the child from the elements, though he doubted they would get more rain. He smiled at his sleeping niece, a gentle and unfamiliar tug pulling his heart. Derek didn't deserve this family, but since he'd taken on the responsibilities of two young 'uns and had bound himself in holy matrimony to their ma, Clay hoped Derek didn't disappoint them as he had his own kin.

Clay stepped away from the wagon and headed back.

As though thoughts of the man conjured him up like an evil spell, Derek strode from the hotel entrance. Clay changed course but soon felt Derek's staying hand on his shoulder.

"Clay—"

"We haven't anything more to discuss. I just put Christa down in the wagon. Now leave me be."

"We have a good deal to discuss yet." Derek pulled Clay around to face him. Though his action wasn't rough and no one stood nearby to witness it, Clay nevertheless grew livid. Derek treated him as if he were still a boy. "You can't keep up this habit of running off before giving me a chance to set things right."

"You ended any chance of that when you left with our maps to the silver," Clay shot back in a fierce whisper.

Derek darted an anxious glance around the area. "I wish you'd keep quiet about that. Mark my words, one day someone'll overhear, and that'll be the end of Pa's legacy for all of us." He ran a hand through his unkempt hair, a few shades darker than Clay's but just as thick and long. Penny had trimmed their hair before the wedding, but both men kept it touching the base of their necks, and both were now clean-shaven. The similarity in mannerisms rankled.

"You didn't care how it affected us back then, me and Linda," Clay argued. "You wanted the full pot. Wanted to rob us blind and take all of what was coming to us."

"And I told you, I'm sorry. I scarce got a wink of sleep the entire time. I felt so ridden with guilt 'cause of all I'd done." Derek's jaw clenched, a sign of his frustration. "Can't you let the past go? If you can't forgive me for my sake, do it for Ma. She'd be sick at heart to have seen us in strife. You know all she wished for us was to live in harmony."

"How dare you bring up Ma to me," Clay seethed between clenched teeth, though he kept his voice low so as not to rouse interest should anyone exit one of the buildings. "You haven't any place to talk about her or her desires! She begged you to come back in her letter, and you wouldn't budge. The illness took her life, but you broke her heart long before that. She wanted you with her at the end, and you were just too selfish and stubborn to honor her dying wish."

"We've been over all this before." Derek's eyes flashed a warning. "I couldn't just up and leave my job. I was the one earning the money for her medicine and your keep, if you'll recall. By the time I made it home, it was too late."

"All just another passel of excuses. You could've been there had you wanted to. You could've found a way."

Derek grabbed Clay's other arm hard as if he might shake him, then relented, and threw both his arms loose from his hold. His action seemed born more from frustration than anger, though in the scant light, it was difficult to read his face. "I've made my fair share of mistakes, Clay. Never said otherwise. Plenty I wish I could take back. But I can't, just like I can't turn back the sun and change what's already been. All I can do is promise I'll do my part to change things for the better. It's what Ma would've wanted."

Clay glared at him. "Don't give me any of your empty oaths. I've had enough to last a lifetime." He turned on his heel, moved away, then whipped around again. "Oh, and just so there's no misunderstanding—once I turned sixteen, I took a job at the mercantile. Old Mr. Dougherty let me bunk in the storeroom there. I never took one red cent of your money, not since I became old enough to get out from under Mrs.

Harper's stingy thumb. Anything I needed, I earned myself."

The satisfaction he should feel to see the confused hurt sweep across Derek's face bypassed him. A twinge of remorse tugged his conscience instead.

"Where'd the money go then?"

Derek's low query stiffened Clay's backbone. The money. Of course. Of all Clay had said, Derek's greed would pick up only on that. "I imagine Mrs. Harper hoarded it away. She sure never spent a penny she didn't have to. Maybe if you leave bright and early tomorrow, you can hightail it back to Missouri and reclaim the money by week's end. That's all you're after anyway. Reclaiming fortunes that are 'rightfully yours.'"

Derek sighed wearily. "How long you plannin' on making me pay for what I did, Clay? How long till we can put this behind us?"

"How long till east meets west? Figuratively speaking, that is."

Derek's eyes went dull as he seemed to recall their old lesson. "It doesn't."

"At least you recall some of what Ma taught us. And so, you have your answer."

This time when Clay turned to leave, Derek didn't stop him.

❧

Clay walked for a good hour from one short end of Silverton to the other, then back again. Pacing the boardwalks. Caged like a wildcat, though the mining town had no jailhouse or bars and was about as much in the wilderness as a man could get without baking to death in the dry, barren desert farther west, near Carson's Sink. He should jump on the horse he'd purchased for this trip and ride away beneath the bright light of the moon, leaving his brother far behind. But he knew he wouldn't go. Travel was dangerous at night, and he wouldn't risk his horse breaking a leg in a gopher hole. . .or chance running across a pack of hungry coyotes.

The last thought surfaced as the beasts' mournful howls wavered a dirge beyond the hills west, raising the fine hairs on the back of Clay's neck. Traveling at night was no option. Come morning, he doubted he would leave this last place he wished to stay, either. New bait kept him trapped: news of the woman whose life he'd helped save and news of the woman whose life he'd helped destroy. Or tried to, by omission of his words.

Clay hung his head and stared at the planks beneath his boots, wishing he could slink between their cracks as shame wormed inside him. He hadn't maligned Linda's character with barbs as Derek had, but he'd done nothing to end his brother's cruelty, either. He'd given his half sister his own share of resentful looks, making sure she knew he also detested her existence, so suddenly sprung upon them through their pa's letter. But after thinking on it, he'd realized that wasn't true. What he detested was his pa's lifetime of lies and manipulations.

Once, when Clay had been little more than a tot, his pa had left for a stretch of months. That must have been when he'd first gone west and associated with Linda's ma. Then when Clay was a boy, sitting on the floor by the hearth with a book, his father left again, bestowing no more than one of his usual disgusted glares upon Clay before slamming the door shut behind himself. Clay never laid eyes on the man again. He'd felt closer ties to his gentle mother than to his stern father so hadn't missed his presence. Some of his peers taunted that Clay was too soft and refined for a boy, but once his ma died, all softness and gentleness went with her. His heart hardened to iron, and he reckoned his soul turned to ice.

On that frozen winter morning, four years after his pa and later Derek had left them, Clay cursed the world that robbed him of his entire family. He became the man his pa claimed he would never be. Hardened. Tough. And while he held his ma's frail, lifeless body in his arms, he cried his last tears and turned his back on what she'd always held closest and dearest to her heart—her faith in God.

But since finding the injured young woman in the desert, he'd begun to feel his heart thaw, had begun to *feel* again.

Tinny music from the dance hall jangled Clay into awareness and away from painful memories as the player piano went into its reel. Shouts of appreciation from the men soon followed, and Clay reckoned that Beulah was performing one of her numbers. The bawdy dancing at times embarrassed him, he'd never been skilled at poker, and the drink made him feel awful come sunup. His ma had been justified in warning him to stay away from such places, and he'd soon discovered he preferred his boyhood habit of reading a good book beside a crackling fire to a night of carousing and losing what little money he'd earned. But on the day he discovered Derek had stolen his part of the map, Clay had reverted to old ways. In his anger-filled ramblings, he'd confided in Beulah, who bore a resemblance to Linda to such a degree that Clay, inebriated though he'd been, soon found himself apologizing to the dance-hall girl for every evil under the sun. Beulah patiently listened, telling him that she wasn't Linda while offering kind advice that Clay planned to take when next he met up with his half sister. Incredible that she'd returned to Silverton, though why she would bother after the grief they'd caused her, he couldn't imagine.

He stared at the swinging doors, the area lit up with gaslights beyond. Maybe Beulah could help him make sense of his current situation by letting him talk it through.

He took a step in that direction, then stopped. The burning temptation to lose his discouragement and anger in cards and drink might reemerge should he walk through those doors and seek her out. And he'd invited enough trouble for one day.

"Mr. Burke?"

He turned at the sound of Shorty's voice and eyed the towheaded lad, still too young for whiskers but unusually tall for fourteen years, just a head shorter than Clay's own six feet. Clay was told the misnomer fit the boy when he was a skinny young 'un; only these past two years he'd shot up like a thick, burly sprout.

"Mrs. Burke asked me to tell you she's lookin' for you but said no need t' hurry if you was busy."

The title stunned Clay a moment until he associated Penny's name with it.

"Thanks, Shorty. Did you tend my horse?"

"He's at the livery, all brushed down and fed." The boy grinned. "You gonna name him? Or leave him nameless like the other Mr. Burke done his?"

Clay assumed Shorty had witnessed his animosity toward Derek not to address him as his brother.

"Don't know, Shorty. I imagine I will."

"Deputy Michaels says you gotta think long and hard on a name befittin' the horse's personality. He's a right smart man, though I ain't ever heard the deputy call his horse a name, either. I reckon if I ever get me enough money to buy a horse, I'll name him Nugget though, cause that's the day when I'll find me some gold."

Reminded of Shorty's due, Clay pulled a coin from his pocket to give the boy for his help. "Silverton has a lawman?" He was surprised that during the one day he'd been absent, the town had found someone to keep the peace.

"No, sir. He comes from some town east of here with Mrs. Michaels. Ain't for sure how long they be stayin'."

Yet another lady to brave the squalid lodging of Silverton? Clay wished her well. That thought led to the young woman he'd brought to town, and he handed the penny to Shorty, then retraced his steps to the hotel.

He met his sister-in-law coming out of the cubicle. "I'll want to be hearin' all of it," she greeted. "How did she get those burns on her hands?"

"You and I both would like the answer to that." He shook his head, flummoxed. "One minute she wasn't there; the next she was."

"Have you taken to the whiskey?" She peered closely at him.

He held up his hands. "I'm stone sober and plan on staying that way."

"Humph. A good thing, too. You don't need any of that devil's brew to muddle your mind further."

"My mind wasn't muddled. It had just rained. When the sun broke out, there was a mist. The valley was empty. Next thing I know, I'm watching that woman in there stumble toward me. I haven't the vaguest notion where she came from."

"She didn't get those burns while she was with you?"

Clay drew himself up. "Meaning?" That Penny might have so low an opinion of him as to think he would physically harm a woman stung.

"Wipe that wounded look off your face, brother. I meant no slur by my speaking. I only thought you'd been witness to what happened."

Mollified, he calmed. Ever since his quarrel with Derek, he felt about as inept at seeing into the heart of the matter as a blind rooster at dawn. "She was that way when I found her."

"Her burns are bad. I'm not certain my remedies will help, but I did all I could. Poor lass. If she uses her hands again, it'll be a miracle." She smiled. "But then, God's in the business of those, isn't He now?"

"I wouldn't know." Smiling, Clay kept his tone light. "May I see her?"

"She hasn't stirred from sleep."

"Isn't it unusual for her to be out cold for so long?"

"I have no way of knowing. I've no experience with anything of this sort."

Clay sighed. "I wish a doctor would arrive on the next stagecoach."

"If you'd not run off as you did and found her, I imagine she'd be dead. You were a godsend."

"Me?" He laughed caustically. "You believe God sent me?"

"Aye. Laugh if you choose, but I believe He wanted her saved. By you."

"Is that what you're trying to do for me, Penny? Save my soul?" He knew she meant the words differently but couldn't resist the question, since for weeks he'd endured similar remarks. "Just as Derek is alleged to have had some sort of divine awakening, though I have my doubts about that, you think I should undergo one, too. Is that what you're aiming for? Let me save you the trouble. I heard a heap of preaching from our ma when I was a boy, and I know about God, but in the end, her faith didn't save her from dying in one of the most agonizing ways I ever saw a body die."

"I lost my mother at an early age, too, Clay." Her tone gentled but remained firm. " 'Tis a grievous choice to let a loved one's death sour your own life. Is that what your ma would have wanted? For you to turn a cold shoulder to the ways she held so dear?" Penny's words made him squirm inside, though outwardly he remained as stiff as the taut canvas. "I only want for you happiness and to know serenity. Derek feels the same."

"Yeah, well he sure has a peculiar way of showing it." Unnerved that she so accurately identified his torment, his inability to find peace or lasting contentment, Clay moved past her into the cubicle. He didn't wish to argue with his sister-in-law as he had with Derek, and he needed to find solitude before he began a rant.

The woman on the hide lay still as death, her skin almost as gray as pale ash, though most of the smudges had been cleansed from her face. Her lashes, a shade lighter than the soot in her hair, rested in feathery crescents against smooth cheeks. Both hands had been bound in clean, white linen and lay helpless at her sides.

His annoyance toward his family forgotten, pity tugged at his heart, and he lowered himself to the ground beside her. He took the liberty of running his fingertips along her arm, where her blackened sleeve met the bandage. "Who are you?" He whispered his thoughts aloud. "And what calamity put you in such a state as this?" He shook his head sadly.

Her thick lashes flickered. Her eyes rolled to and fro beneath thin lids, restless, and she opened them. Clay felt struck anew as he stared into fever-bright orbs of tawny gold flecked with the palest green.

two

"Who. . ." Her throat felt raw, tight. She struggled to swallow, but that made it worse. "Who are you?" Her words came out husky, grating, unlike her usual quiet voice.

She didn't know the handsome face of the man who sat close, striking yet quiet, his deep blue eyes intent on her own, his fingertips on her arm. At the same time, a pinpoint of light pierced her bleary mind. As though realizing he took the liberty, he moved his hand away.

"I know you," she whispered in surprise. "How?" She tried to lift her head and groaned, her curiosity at his presence crumbling away as pain more horrible than anything she'd known wrenched through her limbs and hands. "Oh. . ." A fierce ache throbbed along the back of her scalp, and she dropped back to rest on what felt like fur. Lifting her arms as much as her feeble strength allowed, she stared in horrified confusion at the material wrapped like thick butterfly cocoons around each hand and wrist, halfway up her elbows.

"You're safe in Silverton. In a hotel room, if you can call it that." The man spoke in a quiet voice that somehow soothed. She heard the sound of liquid being stirred. "Here. You need this."

A smooth dipper touched her lips. Something cool and wet dribbled from the ladle and onto her neck. It felt heavenly, and she endured another wave of pain to lift her head and drink what he held. She emptied the dipper of water, and he brought another.

"You have a name?" he asked once she'd taken her fill.

She lay back against the pillow and puckered her brow, trying to think beyond the strange dream to which she'd awakened. A nightmare, in that she lay wounded, yet oddly pleasant because of the handsome and kind stranger who tended her.

"Meagan. I—my name's Meagan. What happened?"

"I had hoped you could tell me."

"What?" She stared in confusion.

He motioned with his hand toward her blanketed body. "How is it you came to be in such a state?"

"I. . .don't know." She grew anxious and more confused once she realized her current situation and that she wore nothing but her chemise beneath the fur coverlet. Surely he hadn't removed her other clothing! Why could she not remember?

"You don't know?"

His disbelieving words pulled Meagan from her own stunned thoughts. He looked at her as if she'd sprouted buffalo horns. She felt as if maybe she had, with the manner in which her skull ached, and realized she must have hit it on something. She groaned as the throbbing increased when she moved her head. The lumpy support beneath her neck smelled of damp animal fur. Not a pillow of feathers, like her own, its soft bristles lightly scratched her nape.

"I can't recall."

"You don't recall wandering alone out in the middle of nowhere?"

"No." She drew her brows together. Even that made her head hurt. She tried to think beyond the pain, to form her words more clearly. "You must be mistaken. Why would I do such a thing?"

"You tell me." He regarded her as if he wasn't sure whether to believe her or not.

"Last I recall I was with. . .Ma and Wayne." She wished to

say her words with force, insistent, but they came slow and slurred. "I wanna see her."

A fuzzy memory tickled her mind; she shoved it away, the pain increasing. Her mother would set things to rights once she swept in with her no-nonsense attitude and scattered all of Meagan's qualms to the wind. She had a way of getting to the heart of a problem with her good sense that flustered Meagan's spirited nature at times.

The stranger continued to stare, this time with a blank look Meagan couldn't identify. "Is Wayne your husband?"

"My brother."

"And your pa is. . .?"

"Stepfather." She struggled to think. "Landon McClinton. He's not here." Odd she should know that, though she had no idea why. Nor could she recollect just where he was.

"So it's your mother, your brother, and yourself?"

His direct questions now seemed invasive.

"You a lawman?"

"No."

"A doctor?"

"No, not one of them either."

"Then why are you so interested in my personal doings?"

The muscle in his jaw jerked, as if she'd taken him by surprise. "I suppose it's because I'm the man who found you."

"Found me?"

"Wandering in a high-desert valley hours west of here. In the hot afternoon sun," he said slowly, as though talking to an invalid. "You were in a bad way." By the careful manner in which his gaze moved along her covered form, she imagined she still was.

"I can't recall. Hurts too much." The effort to try to make sense of what he said made her head pound. Feeling the black mist of blessed unawareness begin to wrap silky nothingness around her again, she fought against succumbing.

"Could you please ask Ma to come?"

He hesitated too long for what shred of comfort she had left.

"She's not here," he said at last.

"She didn't come with you? Then where—?"

"I don't know."

"Don't know? Or won't tell me?" Her whisper bordered on hysteria. His impossible words made no sense. How could this man not know where her ma was? "Is she hurt? And Wayne. Is he hurt, too?"

"I honestly don't know where your family is or what condition they're in."

"But how come? If you found me like you said? They must've been close."

"I'm upsetting you. Don't mean to." He began to push himself up from the ground. "I'll leave you to get some rest."

"No—wait!" She raised her arm, the linen wad making contact with his chest. She winced as pain jarred through her hand, and she lowered it. "Don't go. Please. . .not yet."

The stranger stared, plainly confused by her request, but Meagan felt more anxious about being left helpless and alone in an unfamiliar place than about having her rescuer nearby. He seemed thoughtful enough, considering. The curtain of fog pushed across her mind in its relentless sweep; later she would insist on answers. Right now, she only wanted to lose herself again to empty blackness and lessen the pain.

"Just till I sleep," she pleaded, her words barely heard.

"All right." He settled back down. "You rest. I'll stay."

"Promise?"

"Yes."

She parted her lips to thank him, but the effort suddenly seemed too great. His kind eyes, a deep, serene blue, were the last thing she remembered before she closed heavy lids and the coveted mist wrapped around her once more.

&

"Who you reckon she is?"

"Maybe a princess!" Younger than the first, the second childish voice whispered the words in delighted awe.

"You're such a numskull. A princess? In Silverton?"

"Pa calls Mama his Indian princess sometimes. And don't be callin' me names, Livvie, or I'll tell."

"Not if you want me to teach you to play Grandda's mouth organ, you won't. . .I wonder how she got so much soot on her."

"Maybe it's gunpowder."

"Why would she dump gunpowder in her hair?"

"Dunno."

"Uncle Clay told Mama it looked like she'd been in a fire. That's why her hands got all burnt. He reckoned she used them to put it out."

Meagan did feel as if she'd been set afire, her mind in a smoky haze, but her first worry that Indians captured and tortured her eased as she listened to the children talk. They spoke English, with a gentle, foreign lilt to their words, though at times their speech sounded as western as other emigrants. Her stepfather often told her ma how dangerous native tribes were to white settlers; she'd never met an Indian, though she'd seen some from a distance. But whoever watched her seemed harmless enough. She remembered the stranger with the quiet voice and serene eyes and wondered if that was the girls' uncle Clay.

Bits and pieces of what the children said and what she remembered came clearer, though scattered. She wished to quench all recollections, somehow knowing ignorance remained a far better choice. Relentless, they slithered forward. . .the intolerable heat of fire searing her skin as she pounded at the ever-rising flames. . .a man's gentle hands and anxious voice imploring her to waken. . .distant, frantic screams that rent at her insides. . . .

"What color you think her hair is?" Small, curious fingers snatched up a hank and rubbed it, making a whispery sound near her ear and putting a halt to the beastly memories. A waft of cool air hit where her neck became exposed. "It isn't dark with red like Mama's or real dark like ours. And it isn't red like Aunt Linda's."

"Nobody's hair is as red as that."

"Aunt Linda's is."

A loud sigh escaped. "Never you mind, Christa."

"The dance-hall lady has red hair, too, I saw it. But hers ain't as bright as Aunt Linda's is."

"Don't let Mama hear you talk. She'd tan our hides good if she knew we peeked inside when no one was watchin'."

Meagan felt gentle tugs to her hair, as if it were being twirled around the same curious fingers. "Under all that ash it looks kinda like the flowers that grow by our stream at home."

"It ain't as yellow as them flowers, but with all them glimmers in it and the lamp shinin' on it, it does look like gold dust I've seen some miners pay merchants with. I reckon there's too much soot and dirt to tell."

"I still say she's a princess, Livvie."

"Then why was she out roamin' the valley all alone with no wagon or horse or nothin' with her? Why wasn't she in a grand coach or a castle keep somewhere with servants?"

"I reckon she was out looking for her prince."

The older girl gave a protesting snort. "That was just a tale Grandda told. It wasn't real. You're six years old now, Christa—old enough to know better."

"There are so princes and princesses! Pa said. He read books his ma made him read when he was a young 'un that told him so. And Grandda said his homeland is full of castle keeps. So there!"

"Hush up and fetch the water so I can wet this here cloth. Mama won't be happy if she comes in and sees we haven't done what she told us to yet."

Meagan's hair fell back against her neck as the child released it. Light footsteps padded the ground, and Meagan heard water splash.

"Careful with that, or you're gonna spill it all before I get a chance to use any!"

"Aw, the pail is heavy, Livvie. Why can't you carry it?"

"Cause Mama told me *I'm* supposed to wet down her face." Her reply came off sounding haughty. "Your job is collecting water."

"Why do you always make me do all the hard work?" A loud *thump* hit the ground as Meagan assumed what was the pail dropped down close to her head. She jerked a bit in surprise. "Did you see that, Livvie?" The smallest girl's words came in an excited whisper. "You reckon she's finally waking up?"

"Dunno." The dull plunk of droplets being wrung into water met her ears the moment before a cool, damp cloth swathed her burning face. "Her skin's not so hot as before. You reckon the fever finally broke and that's why she moved? Mama'll be pleased."

"Uncle Clay, too. He's always askin' how she is."

As they continued chattering in hushed whispers, the memory of her quandary unfolded inside Meagan's mind. Her uncertainties returned, riding in on a fresh wave of pain. Her eyelids flickered, and she opened them. The midnight dark eyes of one of the girls, inches away and staring into her own, gave her a sudden fright.

She gasped. The child let out a squeal of shock and jumped back.

"Oh! You are awake. Christa, run and get Mama. Hurry!"

Light footsteps shuffled off at a rapid pace.

"What happened?" Meagan forced her voice to work, rusty with disuse.

"You mean you don't remember nothin'? Not the fire? Or your hands getting burnt? Or Uncle Clay findin' you in the desert?"

Meagan closed her eyes against the child's innocent questions, desperate to remain unaware, wishing she could retrieve her query. But the bits and pieces stitched together into a relentless, gruesome pattern, and Meagan could no longer hold them back.

Those men. . .the fire. . .her mama's screams. . .no. . .God, please. . .

"No–o–o!"

The last she rasped in a wail of despair, feeling as if her heart had been cloven in two. She barely noticed the girl back up in slow retreat, her eyes wide with shocked terror.

three

At the heart-stopping cry of anguish, Penny fumbled with the pouch onto which she stitched Shoshone symbols and hissed as she jabbed the needle's point in her skin. Alarmed, Clay set down a month-old copy of a newspaper from another town and met her eyes across the table. She popped her bleeding thumb into her mouth as she rose from the bench. He did likewise. Another shriek ripped from the area where Meagan lay hidden.

"Glory be, she don't sound well," the nearly toothless Jinx muttered. His spoon stilled from stirring the stew with his three fingers—a disability acquired when using black powder while blasting in a mine but not escaping fast enough the first time he'd done so, and the source of his nickname.

Christa appeared in the kitchen entrance, her face pale. Sensing trouble, they hurried out before the child could offer an explanation. Penny reached Meagan's bedside a hair's breadth ahead of Clay.

"Olivia, what happened?" Penny darted a glance to her patient, then took hold of her eldest daughter by the shoulders. The girl looked shaken, her back up against the wall of canvas. "What did you do to make her cry out like that?"

"Nothing, Mama. Honest! Me and Christa was just talking. I was wetting down her face like you told me to. That's all."

Clay glanced at the ten-year-old, noting the big tears that trekked down her cheeks, before he turned his attention to Meagan. She lay on her side curled up in a tight ball, her bandaged hands pressed to her mouth, trying to muffle the hollow sobs that tore from her slight body. She trembled beneath the blanket. The pathetic picture confused Clay and ripped his heart asunder. One other time he had felt such keen sympathy, a mounting urge to protect from all evils—with his ma. Then as now, he stood helpless, stunned.

"What's wrong with her?" He directed his question to Penny, who sank to the ground beside Meagan. "Is she going to be all right?"

"How can I possibly know?" Penny pressed a soothing hand against the woman's limp, smoke-blackened hair near the lump he remembered discovering when he found her. "Are you in a great deal of pain?" she softly addressed Meagan. "I can brew a tea to help."

Meagan offered no reply; if anything, she seemed to burrow further within herself.

"Leave me alone with her, Clay."

"I'm not going anywhere."

Penny turned at his staunch declaration, her eyes sympathetic. "I need to examine her burns and make certain they've not gone septic."

"I can help."

"No, it wouldn't be fitting. She has injuries besides those on her hands."

At a loss, he glanced at the back of Meagan's head. It seemed so vulnerable and forlorn against the wool-stuffed hide of elk Penny had stitched up for a pillow. Though he knew he must give Penny the privacy needed, he delayed, not wanting to leave Meagan's side. How could he explain this odd connection he felt for the defenseless woman, when he had little cause to care so strongly? All he knew was her given name, for crying out loud, yet somehow she'd become more to him than a stranger in need.

"Clay," Penny persisted.

"All right. Have one of the girls fetch me if you need me for anything."

"I will."

"I mean *anything*."

"You'll be the first person I seek."

With a nod to Penny, he left the cubicle.

"Clay? Can you spare a moment?"

He tensed at the question issued from his right, but not because he didn't want to talk with his half sister. On the contrary; he'd been wishing to speak with her for days, ever since the night he returned to Silverton with Meagan, and more so since he'd discovered Linda was the new Mrs. Michaels. But where Linda was, Kurt and often Derek lurked nearby. A surprise to Clay, given that over a month ago, Derek had treated their newly discovered half sister as his mortal enemy. Yet he seemed to have attained a good pal in Linda's deputy husband. Clay often noticed the two conversing and laughing together, which didn't say much for Kurt's good judgment. Being a lawman, couldn't he perceive what a black-hearted scoundrel Derek was? Or was Clay the only soul alive who could see past his brother's recent pretense of turning over a new leaf?

He turned, grateful to see Linda stood alone. "You've been quiet these days." He attempted a smile but felt awkward. Guilt still ate away at his conscience. He harbored no doubts that this woman was blood kin. She had their pa's determined jaw and piercing gray eyes. The color reminded him of silver nuggets, while Meagan's shimmered as if they contained flecks of the purest gold.

Where did that come from?

Such a sudden and familiar thought linked to the woman in the next room flabbergasted him. Linda self-consciously patted her flame red locks. "Have I got a cocklebur in my hair or something?"

"Sorry." Clay broke off from staring and glanced at his boot tips. "Actually I'm sorry for a whole lot of things." Sheepish, he raised his eyes to hers. "Can we go somewhere and talk?"

Her smile seemed as clumsy as he felt. "I was hoping you would ask."

Clay scanned the area, wondering where to go for privacy. Jinx was still in the kitchen, cooking up the noontime meal—likely stew of whatever small mammal he could find to fill the pot since he never made anything else—and the hotel, usually empty this time of day, crawled with men talking in huddles, he assumed about the latest news.

"We could go for a walk," Linda suggested.

"Sounds like a good idea." Clay led the way in relief that she'd made the suggestion and opened the door. He hesitated before going through, stepping aside to let her precede him. Her brows lifted in surprise as she walked ahead.

"My ma didn't raise a complete oaf. Besides the daily schooling, she taught me manners. She was a schoolteacher before she married my pa. . .our pa," he corrected.

"I never said—"

"I know," he relented, knowing that his shame was the source of his rapid explanation. He wished this moment of reconciliation had fallen far behind them.

The sun burned overhead, covering everything from ground to tents to their wooden fronts in a bright haze that made him squint. They strolled along the road, facing the range of blue-shadowed mountains looming eastward. Linda swiped at her forehead, which had begun to glisten.

"If it's too hot, we can find shade," Clay offered.

"I'm fine." She sent him another uncertain smile. "I've endured far worse than noonday heat."

"About that." Clay couldn't put off the unavoidable any longer. "I want you to know how sorry I am for the way we treated you when you first arrived. Derek never should have said those things, and I should have done something to stop him."

"It's all right. There wasn't much you could do, I suppose, since he's got a mind of his own." Her voice came soft, almost hard to hear as a wagon burdened down with mining equipment rumbled past. "Like I told Derek when he apologized, I'd just as soon forget it ever happened."

Clay glanced at her in surprise. "Derek apologized? To you?"

"Yes, the moment I returned. He was quite sincere, and I told him the same thing I'm telling you now. Let's let bygones be bygones." She cast a glance at the narrow road and cleared her throat, as if gathering courage. "In thinking on it, I'd like us to get to know one another and become a true family, work together and help one another. I know I'm only your half sister, but—"

"I'd like that," he hurried to assure, sensing her discomfort over what their pa had done. "I never thought much about having a sister, but it might be nice."

She turned a bright smile his way, her first real smile since they'd ventured on their stroll. "I'm so relieved, Clay. Derek will be, too. He's the one who approached me with the idea."

"What idea?"

"Why, to leave here soon and search for our legacy together, of course."

"No." His reply came swift.

"But. . ." She blinked in confusion. "I thought. . ."

"After all the grief my—our brother caused, I can't risk teaming up with him."

"Then you still plan to search on your own?"

Her words sounded sad, and he winced, hating that once more he was the source of her pain. "Not right away, no. I have business keeping me in Silverton for a while."

"That woman you brought with you?"

He cast a sharp glance her way. "Why would you ask such a question?"

"I just thought. . ." She struggled to find words, her face going redder. "You've shown such an interest in her welfare. I thought you must have known her before."

"I am interested in what happens to her, that much is true. But I never met her before I brought her here." He wished he could get a woman's viewpoint and explain to Linda the strange attachment he felt, almost from the time Meagan fell senseless into his arms, but discussing a virtual stranger with a half sister he had yet to know felt about as uncomfortable as a new wool union suit in July. He returned the subject to smoother territory.

"Once I do search, rest assured, whatever I find, if I find anything, I won't keep to myself. You'll get your fair portion, Linda. I swear it. I won't take what isn't mine. Like Derek did with us."

"Thank you for that."

He nodded, his focus on the distant hills as they walked.

"He's changed, Clay." She laid her hand tentatively against his arm to gain his full attention. "I wouldn't have believed the man I met on first arriving here and the man who returned were the same. Give him a chance to prove it."

Clay's smile was tight. "He seems to have won you over. Your husband, too. But I know him better than the both of you, and I trust him even less."

"I'm sorry you feel that way. I suppose I do understand, given your long association with him." She sighed. "One thing I've learned these short few weeks is that God sometimes works best when situations are at their worst. Good things can come when you least expect them. I'll pray that for you."

He looked at her sharply, never having figured her for being religious. She sounded like Penny. And his ma.

"Kurt and his aunt taught me about God while I was in Jasperville," Linda explained. "Without them helping me along, in so many ways, I wouldn't be here with you now. I'd be an evil letch's prisoner. Or more than likely, dead."

Clay lifted his brows in surprise.

"It's true. I'll tell you about it sometime. Not now."

He sensed the pain was still too raw for her to talk about it. "If you're expecting a miracle, don't waste your prayers on me, Linda. Not that I believe prayer does any good, but if it ever did work, Meagan could use the assistance instead. She's really suffering."

"I have prayed. Kurt and I both. Derek and Penny have joined us in prayer, too."

Clay changed the subject before she could ask him to join in or introduce more conversation about God. "I'm glad we had this chance to talk. I've wanted to for days, but Derek was always hanging around like a persistent hound dog. He and your husband appear to get along well."

"Yes, they do, and I'm so thankful." She smiled. "When I told Kurt about how Derek first treated me, I was afraid he might punch him in the mouth upon meeting him. He was that upset. But it all worked to the good. We were amazed to discover they both have a friend in common—the marshal of the town Kurt hails from. Derek rode through Jasperville several years back and became friends with him."

"Kurt knew Derek as long ago as that?"

"No. Derek and the marshal became friends. Kurt was still pretty much a boy. He did chores for his aunt at her hotel but didn't recollect Derek's ever being there—not till the two men talked and Kurt remembered an incident Derek brought up, when Marshal Wilson taught Derek tricks with his guns. Kurt remembered looking on from a distance and wishing the marshal would teach him." She chuckled fondly.

"He's learned since then, of course. That was near the time he took an interest in becoming a lawman. From what I understand, Derek wasn't yet nineteen, a few years older than Kurt. Marshal Wilson taught Kurt shortly after and, when he was old enough, made him his deputy." She gave a secret sort of smile. "We met while he was doing his duty as a lawman, but I didn't like him much at the time. He soon proved he could be trusted, though. The longer I knew him, the more I began to care."

"He seems like a good man. I'm happy for you, though I'm surprised he isn't with you today. He usually isn't far."

Her skin took on a pretty rose flush. "He's quite protective. We've been through a good deal in the short time we've known each other. But I convinced him to go with Derek to check on Penny's homestead, like Derek asked. Derek also wants to let nearby miners know a man's running the place and he won't tolerate any of the trouble they gave poor Penny. Derek hopes it will further convince those miners to see a lawman involved and that they'll keep shy of the place while it's vacant." She lowered her voice. "Till we figure out what to do about our pa's mine, Derek and Penny can't settle into ranch life."

"Ranch life?" Last he'd heard, Derek was laying tracks for the railroad. Clay ignored an unexpected prickle of offense to learn the two men left without asking Clay to ride along. Not that he would have gone anywhere with his brother, and he had no idea why he should feel insulted the scoundrel hadn't bothered to ask.

"Derek plans to start a ranch when he leaves here. They need the money the mine will bring to buy cattle."

"Good riddance," he muttered under his breath but didn't fail to note her exasperated look, proof she'd heard him.

He was saved any additional comment as a loud hurrah

went up nearby. A crowd of men huddled in front of the livery, all of them keyed up, judging from their expressions. Clay's curiosity got the best of him.

"Come along." He took Linda's arm in a protective gesture and approached the men. "What's all the hullabaloo about?" he greeted. "Another strike?"

"No—just as good, I reckon," a man with blackened teeth answered. "Just got the news by telegraph. It's done."

"What's done?"

"Where ya been, young feller?" a bearded gent with hair that grew as thick on his forearms jovially asked, slapping Clay on the back. "The Union Pacific and Central Pacific met up. I heard tell they pounded a golden spike in Promontory Summit in Utah today. Two days later than planned cause o' bad weather, but who's counting?" He laughed. "Long as it's finally done."

A short stick of a man smiled, tears in his watery blue eyes. "I reckon that means my dear old mother will be a-joinin' me. She said if ever they came up with a way to travel that didn't involve months of crossing by wagon train, she'd come out west."

"It certainly is much anticipated, my lads," a usually quiet miner said. The tall Cornishman had been given the nickname Gentleman George due to his mannerly and precise way of speaking. "I look forward to the prospect of sending for my family, as well."

"No more travel by wagon train," Linda said under her breath, though Clay could hear her. "That surely will be an improvement."

"Uncle Clay," Livvie called, "Aunt Linda!"

Both turned to see Penny's oldest girl race across the street.

"Mama wants you. Christa got stung by somethin', and Mama wants you to come quick."

Clay and Linda hurried with their niece to the hotel. He could hear Christa's squalling before he stepped foot inside. He spotted Penny with her arms around Christa, trying to comfort her squirming child. Christa's arm was reddened and puffy.

"Stay with Meagan," Penny told Linda. "I doona want her left to herself. I'm not sure what ails Christa. From the little I could understand, a flying bug stung her. Likely a bee with the way they've been buzzing around. There must be a hive somewhere close."

"You look as if you could use help calming her," Linda countered.

"Go with Penny," Clay inserted. "I'll stay with Meagan."

Linda nodded, and the two women hurried away with the child. Christa's cries grew fainter, and Clay inhaled a steadying breath. He hated to witness any female's pain, be it girl or woman. He thought of Meagan, wishing he knew how to take her heartache away.

Entering the room, he noticed she still lay huddled in a ball, her back to him. The blanket had fallen away in her struggles, her smoke-blackened chemise now apparent. He walked around to face her and hunched down. Her teary eyes were open, but she didn't acknowledge him, only stared straight ahead. Prickles danced along his spine as he recalled her similar behavior when he'd first found her wandering in the valley.

"Miss?" He pulled the edge of the cover over her chemise, trying not to notice how round and soft her bare shoulder appeared. "Can you hear me?"

She didn't respond and flinched when his fingertips brushed her neck as he pulled his hand from the blanket. He released a weary breath, unable to understand the churning inside his heart. He'd never felt this way about anyone and assumed pity caused such intense feeling. Yet when he was with her, pity was only one layer of what he suffered. If he were to believe Jinx, he might think her a wandering gypsy who'd cast a spell on him. But she neither looked like a gypsy—her skin fair beneath the soot, her hair and eyes dark golden—nor did she wear the gaudy clothes of one. Not that he believed such farfetched tales.

"You're going to be all right," he told the unresponsive woman. Uncertain what to do, he settled into another position, trying to make his long legs comfortable by crossing them. Keeping his touch feather light, he laid his fingertips against the edge of one of her bandages. "I'm not leaving here till you do. I'll help you through whatever it is you're dealing with, however I can. You're not alone—I just wanted you to know that."

She didn't answer, but Clay noticed the tenseness of her jaw slacken and her eyes close, as if in relief. When her breathing grew even and deep, proof that she at last slept, he quietly added, "No, Miss Meagan, there isn't much that'll make me leave Silverton a second time. Not yet. Not the prospect of silver, not being forced to reunite with my black sheep of a brother. I reckon you're stuck with me for a while."

The notion made Clay smile.

❧

Over the next two days, Meagan became more aware of her surroundings each time she woke, but she didn't speak. To do so might break up the dam welling inside, though late at night, when everyone else slept, she allowed hot tears to fall and smothered her sobs in the scratchy pillow. What grieving she did in secret helped, and in sleep, she often escaped memories, but sometimes they slithered into her dreams like vicious serpents, their excruciating bites making her jerk awake with a shock and gasp for breath.

She wavered back and forth between hoping the events

must be some horrid, twisted nightmare and knowing it wasn't so. During the latter times, such desolation filled her soul she wished she could again dissolve into the fog that once held her mind captive, with the hope that it would make the anguish disappear, too.

The woman called Penny often tended her wounded hands and fed her, spooning meat broths into her mouth. She bore Indian blood if her physical appearance and moccasins were anything to judge by, though she wore the clothes of a white woman and spoke with a lilting, European burr Meagan had never heard except from the two little girls. She didn't think her accent originated from any tribe in these parts, though she had no way of knowing. Indian or not, Penny was kind, her quiet ways and gentle hands bringing a measure of bodily comfort. Her two daughters often aided her, and their constant magpie chattering helped Meagan to forget her misery for a time. After their first scare while tending her, Livvie and Christa soon recovered and seemed to enjoy their one-sided conversations with Meagan as she lay silent.

When Penny or her girls weren't near, the man she heard Penny address as Clay kept vigil by Meagan's bedside. Whereas the girls were talkative, Clay was silent, often brooding, though Meagan no longer suffered qualms regarding the tall, dark stranger. He'd exhibited toward her a gentleness she hadn't thought a man capable of—especially when she recalled her more lucid moments and the feel of his muscles like iron as he'd held her against him that first day. She realized she had him to thank for what was left of her life.

From beneath her lashes, she stared at him, hoping he would think she still slept. Whether she should thank him or curse him for his act she couldn't decide.

"I thought you might like something to read to ease the boredom." Penny walked into the room, handing Clay a book.

"It'll help pass the time."

Clay made a sound of protest after he took the large book in his hands and glanced at the cover. "A Bible? I can't—"

"Now then, there's no use tellin' me you haven't the skill to read." She cut him off before he could finish his sentence. "I know otherwise. You mentioned once that you like to do so of an evening. And your mother was a teacher, Derek told me. Considering what little she taught him in the short time he took lessons, I'm certain she spent years teaching you a good sight more."

Clay grumbled. "Don't you have any other books?"

"I haven't a wide supply at present," she answered wryly. "Most of my da's books I left at the shanty before we took our journey—I had no wish to weigh down the wagon. So you'd best reconcile yourself to what's offered."

"This is the only book you have with you?" he insisted.

She crossed her arms over her chest and raised her brows. "I have two others. A McGuffey's reader that Livvie and Christa use and a book of poetry."

"Fine then. I'll take the poetry."

Meagan thought Penny's exasperated sigh might stir the canvas walls. Had she not felt such misery, she might have cracked a smile at Clay's boyish stubbornness.

"Very well. I'll just fetch it then, shall I?"

"I'd appreciate it."

"Humph." She glanced in Meagan's direction, and Meagan closed her eyes. "Has she come around?"

"No. Hasn't moved from that position ever since I came to guard her."

"Guard her?"

"Need I remind you of where we currently reside?"

Penny let out a breath. "You're wise to be so protective, Clay. All sorts make up a town of this nature. Although Mr.

Matthis is kind—and Jinx. They would never cause a lady harm. For most of these men, 'tis been a long while since they've seen a woman. A decent woman. They treat Linda well, to the point of idolatry. And a few give me the same esteem, despite what Shoshone blood I bear, so I imagine Meagan will fare well."

"There are others who think differently."

"Aye. . .there are always others."

At their uneasy manner of speaking, Meagan felt apprehensive. What kind of town had he brought her to?

"I fail to understand why she's not spoken. You said she did so the first night?"

"Not much. She told me her name. That's all that I know about her."

Meagan heard regret in his voice and pondered the cause of it.

"Something dreadful must have happened to the wee lassie to cause her to draw into herself in such a manner." Penny's moccasins made a scuffing sound toward the entrance. "So tragic."

Tragic. Yes. An apt word to describe what remained of her life. Helpless to stop it, Meagan hoped no one could see the tear trickle from beneath her lashes and roll to her temple.

four

Clay saw the tear and held his breath.

Had she been awake this entire time and privy to their conversation? Why should she feign sleep? She'd made it obvious she didn't want to speak these past forty-eight hours; nor had anyone forced her since that first evening when he'd fumbled with his questions and almost brought her to panicked tears. He still winced when he thought about his clumsy behavior. Since then, he had tried to think his words over, testing them before he spoke, not wanting to send her over the brink a second time. He'd heard whispers from a few boarders that she must be a mite touched in the head not to recall all that happened. Likewise, he'd never heard of a person losing part of their memory except in their dotage. Nor had anyone else known of such an occurrence. But neither did he think that Meagan lied about her inability to remember. He hoped those men were wrong and she wasn't loco. His gut told him she was as sane as he.

Clay leaned closer to her. "Meag—Miss?" He just prevented himself from addressing her by her Christian name, not wanting to show disrespect, though that's the only name she'd given and that's how he thought of her. "Are you awake?"

Her lids creased, squeezing the barest fraction tighter, and he realized with some amazement she wanted him to go on thinking she slept, much like Christa or Livvie when they played possum. He considered the matter, wondering if he should continue or just let her be.

"Well now, that's a shame. Mind you, the quiet is nice, but

hour after hour of it can get trying and creep beneath a man's bones—makes him restless to hear another voice. Enough so that he might start talking to himself for company. . . . I suppose I'll just have to fill the air with my own chatter to pass the time. Like as not, hearing me talk can get somewhat monotonous. So I suppose it's a good sight better that you're sleeping and don't have to suffer the tedium. If you were awake, I don't know how you could stand it."

Her eyelashes flickered, but she didn't open her eyes.

Sure now she must be feigning sleep, he went on, "Still, I was hoping you might wake up soon. You've slept the entire day away. My sister-in-law insists that sleep is good for a body, but too much can't be beneficial. Not when you need nourishment, too. Jinx makes some of the finest badger stew this side of the Rockies, not that I've had badger stew elsewhere. But it puts meat on one's bones—not that I think you need meat on your bones, but it couldn't hurt. To help build your strength. Not that I think you're too lean." He quit, realizing he'd bungled his words and said the wrong thing again, but then he saw the corner of her mouth flicker the tiniest bit. That he might make her smile—something he'd never believed possible when the most he'd hoped for was getting her to open her eyes—made his embarrassment drift away, and he grinned.

"Of course then, there's Penny. My sister-in-law. She could use some meat on her bones, I reckon, though not for strength. Oh no, not Penny. She's got an attitude that's strong as a bull's and thrice as stubborn as a mule's." He moved a little closer to her ear, lowering his voice. "Just don't tell her I said so."

Her chapped lips quivered a bit, as if holding back a sign of mirth.

"But she's a good woman owning a heart pure as snow,

though not as cold. Her bones may be little, but there's not a mean one in her body. You can depend on her. She's efficient when it comes to her remedies, wise when it comes to doling out advice. Fact is, plenty of people here care what happens to you, and not just Penny."

"Well now, Clayton. . ."

At the amused lilt of his sister-in-law's voice Clay jumped back a good foot. He tried to cover his loss of composure as she stepped past the curtain. "What are you doing, sneaking up on a person like that?"

"Have a guilty conscience, do you? Huh. If you should wish to see the bearer of an attitude strong as a bull's and thrice as stubborn as a mule's, I'd advise you look in the stream on a clear day and see who be starin' back. Bein' as how my counsel's so wise, I'm assured you'll be takin' it."

This time he didn't mistake the thread of a muffled gasp as Meagan held back a laugh, though she kept her eyes and lips skewed shut. He and Penny shared a quick look. Her smile went wider as she also realized Meagan almost laughed. She looked toward the bed, her brow curious, then to Clay. Before she could open her mouth to query him, he gave a slight shake of his head, still smiling. For some reason he couldn't place, he wanted to let Meagan continue her little game and speak when she was ready. He felt a good deal better knowing they'd given her a dose of happiness, however small, and if her pretense of sleep helped, well then, so be it.

His gaze shifted to Penny's hand. "That the poetry?"

"Aye, it is."

His curiosity piqued at the twinkle in her eyes, he got no further than taking the book, when a multitude of heavy steps from outside drew close.

"Penny, you in there?" Derek's voice came from the other side of the curtain.

She drew it back, her eyes lighting up to see Derek but soon clouding with concern. He hugged her briefly. "Whatever is the matter?"

Derek, Kurt, and another man Clay didn't recognize stood outside. From their tense jaws and sober eyes, Clay knew trouble threatened.

"We need to talk," Kurt said.

They took their conversation to the other side of the curtain.

"On the way from the homestead, we took another route." Derek kept his voice low, but as deep and clear as it was, he may as well have been standing next to Clay. "Wanted to warn any other miners that a man was running the place now. We came upon a shack—what was left of it. Fire burned it."

"Do you suppose it was the same fire Meagan came against?" Penny asked.

Clay shot a glance toward the young woman. Her eyes remained closed, but her wrapped hand moved a fraction.

"Can't say. The shack wasn't empty." Derek's voice sounded grim. "Found two bodies. A woman and a boy. Reckon he was no more than fourteen." He sounded truly regretful about the discovery, which also moved Clay.

"Injuns!" an unfamiliar voice claimed with malice. "They musta done it."

"We haven't had trouble in these parts for some time," Kurt argued. "The tribes that were living here are on reservations now."

"There's always them renegades causing trouble," the stranger staunchly replied. "Can't trust any Injun."

"Just what do you mean by that?" Derek's question weighed heavy with warning.

"Just what I said." By the menacing drawl of the stranger's voice, Clay imagined the man meant Penny.

"Be careful what you say and how you say it," Derek replied, his tone as threatening. "I'd advise you to think on it first, a good long time, before saying anything further."

"You aim on stopping me? I got a right to speak—and I ain't the only one 'round these parts that feels thatta way. So's unless you plan on taking on the whole town, you best think twice before opening your trap in favor of an Injun again."

"Out of respect to my wife, I'll ask you once more to keep your mouth shut."

"Respect?" the stranger sneered. "No one asked you to bring her here."

As the men's words grew more heated with each view aired, Clay hoped Derek had enough sense to take it outside and not start a fight with women present and in danger of getting hurt. He also detested how the scoundrel mistreated Penny.

"Not. . .Indians."

Clay's attention jerked from the argument to Meagan, surprised to hear her small voice amid the growing ruckus. Her eyes were wide open and staring at him.

"Did you say something?" he asked, shocked that she'd actually spoken.

She made a visible effort to swallow. "The men. . .who burned my home. Not Indians."

"That was your home they're talking about?" Dread laced his words. Derek had said they'd found two bodies there.

She nodded, tears glistening in her eyes already red-rimmed from the crying he'd heard each night. Since he'd brought her to Silverton, he bunked outside her cubicle to keep watch. Though his heart had ached to hear her muffled sobs, he'd let her be, figuring she needed time to deal with whatever demons plagued her. Now it appeared as if he would finally learn the cause of her torment.

"Ma," she said. "And Wayne. . .my brother. They. . ." The

tears that brimmed in her eyes ran over, and her body began to tremble.

"Shh. It's all right." He gently clasped her shoulder.

The sound of scuffling and grunting rose from outside the cubicle.

"Derek, no!" Penny cried.

Clay shot a glance at the curtain. It billowed as if someone pushed against it.

"You're safe, and I'm here to make sure it stays that way. But you need to tell the others the truth before a skirmish starts out there."

Like a frightened child, Meagan pulled at her lower lip with her teeth but nodded assent. Clay wrenched the curtain aside. Derek clutched handfuls of the stranger's shirt. Kurt tried to hold back one of Derek's muscled arms, Penny the other.

Clay loudly cleared his throat.

Penny looked at him in surprise, as did Kurt.

"If you can stop quarrelling long enough to listen, there's something you should hear." Clay stepped aside to let them enter. As if frozen in place, Derek remained fixed a moment, then released the man's shirt with a little push.

"Don't ever talk that way about my wife again," Derek warned in a low growl before striding into the cubicle. Anxiety plainly written on her face, Penny followed, but the stranger gave them a disgusted scowl and left.

"Who was he?" Penny asked Derek, touching his arm.

"No one." He drew her close to his side. "Don't worry about it. He won't cause further harm."

"Unfortunate as it is, his views are shared by other men here," Kurt reminded grimly.

"Well, we're not leaving." Derek's eyes blazed. "Not till we're ready. And if they try and force us, they'll wish they hadn't."

"Violence isn't the answer," Penny inserted softly. "It just breeds more violence, which in turn breeds more, and it goes on and on, a never-ending circle of fighting and death."

Clay watched his brother's face relax and marveled that Penny had such an effect on him. "I know what you're saying is true. I just wish. . ."

"That we could all get along?" she finished for him. "I agree." She directed her attention to Clay. "It will be a blessed day when we can get along peaceably and put old hurts behind us. It took many years for me to come to that knowledge, but I'm thankful it didn't come too late."

Clay didn't doubt the topic of conversation had altered from the stranger's threats to the clash between himself and Derek. He chose to ignore Penny and looked instead at Meagan, who regarded each of their faces with uncertainty. She had managed to sit up and had turned her eyes his way. Lines of doubt dissolved from her face, and her features relaxed. She looked at him much as Derek had at Penny when her words calmed him, and Clay realized with surprise he had earned Meagan's trust. Though she recalled little, maybe she did remember him finding her in the wilderness.

He gave her a faint smile and nod of encouragement.

Meagan closed her eyes, clearly apprehensive of facing what must be said. Clay knew it couldn't be easy for her.

"Those men weren't Indians," she said. "The men you were talking about. There were two of them. I—I don't know who they were. Strangers I'd never seen."

"Do you remember what they look like?" Kurt assumed a quiet but firm official attitude Clay had begun to associate with the deputy when speaking of matters pertaining to the law.

She shook her head. "No, I. . .they had beards. One stood taller. . .that's all I can recall."

Her description could apply to over half the men in

Silverton. Still, Clay had an uneasy feeling she held something back.

"I need you to tell me all that happened," Kurt insisted. "Did they set fire to the shack?"

"I don't remember." She stared at the bandages covering her hands, her breathing more labored.

Kurt blinked, clearly not expecting such an answer. "You remember the men but not what they did?"

"No." Her reply came swift. "I still can barely recall anything. It hurts my head to think."

"If you saw them again, could you identify them?" Kurt persisted.

"I. . .don't know." She pressed her swathed hands to each side of her head. "I saw them for such a short time."

"Did they say anything? Maybe call each other by name? Any information you can give might help."

"I don't know!" She slightly rocked in her agitation. "Please, that's all I can tell you."

Kurt seemed just as upset. Penny shook her head for him to stop when he would have questioned Meagan further. He closed his mouth before he could say whatever he'd planned to and sighed.

"You'll let me know the minute you recall anything? No lawman resides in Silverton. But since I'm staying awhile, I'll look into this and do all I can to help catch these men."

Meagan nodded, her gaze fixed on the blanket. Kurt and the others moved to leave the room. "Wait!" She looked up. "Please, can you tell me. . .the. . .bodies you found. . ."

"We gave them a proper Christian burial." Derek cut off her need to ask the difficult question. "I spoke over their graves, asking the Lord to carry them through to the other side. And the deputy here read a verse or two from the Good Book he carries."

Astounded, Clay listened to his brother show kindness toward a stranger, trying to ease her pain. He spoke about God as if he knew Him. Derek had claimed a newfound relationship with the Lord upon his return to Silverton, but Clay hadn't believed him.

"Were they friends of yours?" Kurt lowered his voice to a respectful level for the dead.

"My family. Thank you. . .for all you both did." On the tail end of her mournful whisper, silent tears dripped down her cheeks.

The sight stirred Clay; the sudden urge to take her in his arms and comfort her nearly overwhelmed him. He looked at the others, who stared at Meagan, clearly stunned and uncomfortable by her admission.

"Sorry to hear that, miss," Derek added, his tone gentle. "We also sang what we know of 'Shall We Gather at the River.' Seemed appropriate, bein' as how the Humboldt runs so close."

"Ma would've liked that." Meagan brushed away the tears with the back of her hand. "She liked to sing."

An uncomfortable silence fell upon the room. No one knew quite what to say.

Recalling his need for solitude after his ma died, Clay took charge, herding the others out of the room with him and assuring Meagan that someone would be in to look after her later. The men walked ahead, deep in discussion. Penny walked alongside Clay.

"That was very astute of you," she whispered, as if surprised.

"I'm not a complete boor," he argued. "I've been in her place."

"Aye. Be thankful you still have your brother."

His defenses charged ahead. "Penny, that subject is dead and buried. I'm not keen on resurrecting it and hashing this out with you again. No good'll come of it."

"At least you have a second chance to do some good," she insisted, turning to face him. "But that poor wee lassie in there will never be talkin' to her brother again. The only thing 'dead and buried' for her is her family."

Clay winced. "Sorry. A poor choice of words on my part, considering the situation."

"Don't be apologizing on my account. But hear my counsel, dear brother, not only with your ears, but with your heart as well." She grasped his forearm, as if concerned he might flee before she spoke, though he hadn't moved a muscle. "My dear da used to say, 'Life is too short to be shouldering a lifetime of grudges. 'Tis a burden that's utterly useless, has no worth, and gives its bearer naught but a great deal of suffering.' A lesson I myself had to learn, and you're far too intelligent a man to carry such a burden on your shoulders."

He managed a wry grin. Even when she chastised him, she had a way of paying him tribute. At one point, before she married his brother, Clay had vied for her affection, never having met anyone like Penny—intrigued by the petite but strong woman who bore a mix of Scots and Shoshone blood. Either his overtures were far too subtle or he'd had no chance to begin with, and on the occasions he glimpsed her alone with Derek, he presumed it was the latter. In the short time since she'd become Derek's wife, Clay had uprooted his newly budded affection for his sister-in-law, thankful it had been given no chance to grow and she'd never suspected his earlier feelings. Instead he showed her the fond respect a brother should. Likewise, she treated him as the little brother she'd never had. But at times, he thought she might drive him to drink, and if he weren't so infuriated with Derek, he could almost pity his brother, as often as she tried to mend the unmendable—neither action a course Clay wished to travel.

"You can't rescue everyone, Penny." He kept his words calm. "Some are lost causes."

"Och, there is no such thing," she scoffed. "I'm a wee bit on the inquisitive side. Ask Derek if you've not yet discovered this fault of mine. But fault or no, I'll do all I can to help my family, which is what you are. 'Tis the way I was raised and the example my parents gave. I can do no less. So you may as well accustom yourself to my involvement."

He gave her an exasperated smile, letting out a harsh laugh mingled with a sigh. "I suppose it'll do me no good to try and ignore you, and you will just have to be my cross to bear?"

"God can take away *all* your burdens, if you'll allow it, Clay. Not just the ones of which I spoke. But those you tell no one about."

Her tone serious again, she spoke as his ma might have. Suddenly Clay wanted escape. "Could be," he said, not really believing it. "Whatever the case, I just now realized I should go to the livery and check on my horse before it thinks its owner abandoned it." A pathetic excuse, but he moved away before she could tell him so.

"Run if you wish it, but He's not far behind. And when you're weary of running, He'll always be there to turn back to."

"I'm not running from anything or anybody," he muttered under his breath. That she should think he was behaving like a coward made him want to shout out his defense to any and all who would listen. He quickened his stride, giving himself no cause to regret such actions.

❧

Meagan felt warm breath laced with some tangy herb—rosemary, perhaps—brush her face.

"Christa, don't get so close," Livvie chastened. "Mama said we wasn't to touch her. Just watch her till she comes back."

Meagan waited until she heard the soft rustles of the little girl's moccasins and dress scoot against the ground before she opened her eyes. She didn't want to alarm Christa like she'd done with Livvie that first day she'd awakened with the girls in the room.

"Oh—you're awake!" Christa's grin seemed uncertain. Meagan knew the children regarded her with some fear, in part due to the mystery surrounding her—a mystery that she could scarce remember in its entirety. She managed a smile, hoping to reassure the pair she wasn't an evil witch come to harm them.

"Hello." Her voice still sounded husky, and her throat felt raw, likely from the weeping, but after using it the past few days, her words didn't come as feeble as before.

"You *can* talk!" Christa's smile widened, and she clapped her hands together. Had the room not been so small, Meagan supposed the child might have danced about. She knew the youngest of the two to be six, from what Livvie had said, but couldn't help thinking she looked much too tiny and frail. She seemed closer to four.

"Course she can talk," Livvie said with an exasperated big-sister attitude Meagan had often used on her brother. "How else you think Uncle Clay learned her name?"

"Well, she never talked to us," Christa defended.

"She did to me."

"But not me!"

"No, I never have, have I?" Meagan's smile grew sheepish.

Any reserve Christa might have shown evaporated like mist in midmorning. She scooted closer until her knees pressed against Meagan's side. "How come you didn't say nothin' then?"

"I suppose it was owin' to the fact it was too hard. At first."

"Huh?" Christa cocked her head.

" 'Cause of the F-I-R-E," Livvie whispered near her sister.

"Fur?"

Livvie rolled her eyes. "No, dummy." She cupped her hand around Christa's ear and whispered something into it. The small girl's eyes grew bigger.

"Oh."

Uncomfortable with the bend of the conversation and the way the pair acted, Meagan moved to sit up, using her bandaged hands as leverage. They still stung and throbbed dreadfully, though the paste of herbs Penny slathered on them twice a day helped ease the pain. Her hair, matted and stinking of smoke, made her stomach turn, and her damp body and clothing, stinking of sweat, felt just as repulsive.

Looking at the two girls, their faces curious and expectant as if waiting to see what she might do next, Meagan searched for something to say. No words came to mind.

"You like horses?" Livvie asked.

"Horses?" The question took her aback. "I suppose."

"Pa said me and Christa can think up a name for his. He never named her, don't know why. Uncle Clay didn't name his, either. But me and Christa can't agree, so maybe you can help. She wants a name like those from the tales our Grandda told—and I want a name more befittin' a horse in the West."

At the mention of Clay's name, pleasant warmth unfurled inside Meagan, and she remembered the tall man with the clear eyes and soothing voice who'd taken care of her so often during Penny's absences. She tried to cover her interest, hoping the girls were too young to note her reaction, and posed a question to aid them with their quandary. "Will your. . .Uncle Clay. . ." She stumbled over the use of his given name. "Will he also need a name for his horse?"

The two girls looked at each other. "I reckon he will," the oldest agreed.

"That would solve your problem then. Each of you could name a horse."

"Why didn't we think of that?" Livvie exclaimed, looking at her sister.

"Let's ask him!" A shine brought Christa's dark eyes to life. They lifted higher just as Meagan heard the curtain draw back. Christa smiled as if it were Christmas. "Uncle Clay! We was just talkin' about you."

"Were you now?"

She jumped up from the ground and covered the short distance to him, wrapping her arms around his middle as if she hadn't seen him in months. He chuckled, his hands going under her arms as he lifted her high. "Lower your voice, sweet potato," he chided, "or the whole town'll hear."

Christa must have barely weighed as much as a small sack of potatoes, but Meagan was sure if she weighed more than a barrel of nails, Clay would have lifted her with the same ease. He may have been on the lean side, but his arms and chest were solid with muscle and strong. She felt her face warm at the fuzzy memory of being held against him.

"How's our patient? She awake?" He directed his gaze Meagan's way; she was certain her cheeks must be blazing berry red after such thoughts of him.

He looked as if he'd come fresh from the barber. His face was clean-shaven, his hair still damp with a slight curl at the ends. A pleasant aroma of wood smoke and sunshine drifted from him, reminding Meagan of her own disgusting condition. Embarrassed, she almost wished she had thought to slip beneath the cover and feign sleep as she'd done before. His smile came open and honest, offering no criticism, and she managed a feeble one, unable to prevent her lips from turning up when looking at him.

"Good afternoon," he said to her as he set Christa back on her feet.

She nodded in turn.

"How are you feeling?"

"Fairly well, all things considering."

His gaze dropped to one of her bound hands. "I imagine they must still give you a good deal of pain."

She felt awkward discussing her wretched condition. "Penny's cures help. But it'll be nice doing things for myself again and not having to depend on others."

She couldn't read his expression as he turned his head away. He acted guarded, as if he suddenly didn't want to discuss the matter. She hoped her comment hadn't come across as unthankful.

"Not that I'm not beholden to every one of you. I'm grateful for all you've done."

"Do you like the flowers I brought?" Christa asked.

At the child's question, Meagan noticed the spray of yellow, blue, and white wildflowers sitting inside a chipped mug on the ground nearby. A few of the stems hung crooked.

"Mama used the same kind of flowers in her wedding bouquet. She said they made her feel like she was holding sunshine. So, bein' as you can't go outside, I brought some to you." Christa ducked her head, acting shy. Before Meagan could thank her, she went on, "Mr. Matthis said I was silly to pick useless plants that was just gonna wither up anyhow, but Mama said it was fine and he just don't know how womenfolk think."

"As if any man does," Meagan heard Clay mumble.

"Sorry some got broke. That's how I got stung. See?" Christa held up her arm. A pink bump swelled near her elbow. "The flowers was growin' near the livery, and a bee stung me. Jinx said it musta been guardin' the flowers and I didn't ask permission from it to take 'em, but Mama thinks Jinx is full of hogwash."

Clay snorted, abruptly stifling a laugh. Meagan didn't know who Jinx was, except that he made the stews Penny spoon-fed her, and assumed he must be quite the colorful character from the little she'd heard.

She smiled. "I'm awful sorry you got stung, Christa, but I thank you for the flowers. They do brighten up the room."

The girl's smile came just as bright.

"Off with you then," Clay said good-naturedly. "Your mama will be looking for you two."

"Can we name your horse?" Livvie blurted.

"What?" Clay's eyebrows lifted in bewilderment.

"Pa gave us permission to come up with a name for his," Livvie went on, "and Christa wants to name it some silly name. But I want to name it something else."

"Princess Rose is not a silly name!" Christa insisted.

"Is so. Anyhow, Miss Meagan said you might like a name for your horse, too. That way I can name one, and Christa can name the other."

Clay looked at Meagan. Embarrassed, she averted her gaze.

"Well, I can't think of a reason why not. With all that's been going on this past month, I haven't had time to give it much thought." He gave a preoccupied nod. "You can name my horse. On the condition I approve your choice. And Princess Rose won't work. It's a stallion."

Christa looked puzzled.

"A boy horse, dummy," Livvie supplied.

"Stop calling me that!"

"Livvie, you know how your mama feels about name-calling. I think it's time the two of you scoot," Clay urged, pulling back the curtain as a sign for them to go. "I'm sure your mama has more chores for you with suppertime approaching."

" 'Bye, Miss Meagan," Livvie said and hurried through. Clay playfully swatted her backside. She shrieked, then giggled, darting away.

" 'Bye, Miss Meagan," Christa chimed in after her big sister and followed, squealing as Clay tried to do the same to her and she blocked his effort with her tiny hands.

"Hard to believe," Clay said once the children left, "but according to Penny, those two were once leery of strangers, and Christa was shy. Since living in Silverton, they've shed their reserve like old skins. Livvie's bolder, not always a good thing, and Christa's vocabulary has grown by leaps and bounds. It's a wonder those two haven't picked up the vulgarities many of the miners use, though their grammar has gotten worse."

"They're sweet. Christa reminds me of someone I know."

"Oh?"

Meagan smiled, unwilling to admit the child reminded her of herself, especially at that age. Her ma always said she walked with her head in the clouds with all her daydreaming. Thoughts of her ma increased the ache in her heart, and she changed the subject to one more manageable.

"I'm sorry I interfered. I had no right speaking to them about naming your horse, not without talking it over with you. I only hoped to end their quarrel."

"No harm done." Clay chuckled wryly, as if his mind lay elsewhere. "It's a crying shame, but Livvie grows less tolerant of Christa with each day that passes. I imagine all siblings struggle with problems. Especially as they grow older."

Meagan sensed his last words weren't about the girls. They also made her think of Wayne. She couldn't avoid the issue forever but wondered if the pain of loss and burden of guilt would ever ease.

"Mr.—I'm sorry. I don't know how to call you."

"Oversight on my part. Full name's Clayton Thomas Burke. Folks call me Clay. And you're Meagan. . .?"

"Foster. Middle name's Elizabeth." It seemed odd exchanging official introductions; she felt as if she'd known this man her entire lifetime when in reality it must be nearing a week. Ever since she'd opened her eyes and looked into his, she'd felt a keen regard toward him. "You can call me Meagan, bein' that's how everyone knows me."

"Meagan it is." He smiled, his eyes lighting up, and she had the oddest sensation of her insides doing a somersault.

"Thing is. . ." She noted the small croak in her voice that had nothing to do with disuse and cleared her throat. "You've done so much already—finding me, takin' care of me. I know I have no right to ask for anything more, bein' as how I'm nothin' but a stranger. . . . " She hesitated, wondering if he would think she asked too much.

"Go ahead, Meagan. Tell me what's on your mind."

The way he spoke her name—quiet and deep—gave her delicious chills, and she could drown in those eyes of his and be grateful for the experience. "I have a favor I'd like to ask of you. . .Clay. . .that is, if you wouldn't mind."

His ready smile gave her all the encouragement she needed.

five

Clay exited the hotel, his mind so caught up in the last few minutes that he walked right past where Kurt and Derek sat in two chairs in the shade and had to retrace his steps. Most of Silverton's storefronts had no boards laid out for walking, though a few did. Clay surmised the hotel would have done far better to replace their scratchy hides for comfortable beds with feather mattresses than to waste time and expense nailing boards together underfoot, when a man's boots got just as dusty after stepping off them.

Kurt's aunt ran a hotel in Jasperville, and he told Clay that Silverton's public mode of lodging maintained some of the meanest standards he'd come across. The town had sprung up after a recent silver strike and, with more merchants and miners arriving each day, hadn't been in existence long enough for improvements. "A few months," Jinx had said, which by the cook's standards of recording time could mean anywhere from two to twelve months. Clay felt it must be the former, as shabby as the town appeared. All except for the fine boardwalk of smoothed-down planks, of course.

"Clay," Kurt greeted. "Something on your mind?"

"Or someone?" Derek added.

His amused words sparked the memory of his brother ribbing him in the days they got along before Derek left home. He grinned at Clay, and for a fraction of time, Clay wished things could go back to the way they once were. No need telling either man that he pondered the inane use of outside flooring; they might think him as crazy as many assumed Meagan was, and he winced when he recalled the nickname "Mad Meagan" that some of the miners now called her.

"As a matter of fact, I do have something I'd like to discuss." Clay addressed Kurt, planting one boot in the street and propping the other on the edge of the boardwalk. He casually rested his arm against his leg and leaned forward. "Meagan wants to visit the site where her family's buried. As I don't know where that is, I'd like you to come along."

"Be happy to," Kurt replied. "It would also give me the opportunity to take a look around the area, get more of an idea what happened, maybe rustle up some clues."

"I can help there," Derek added. "Don't plan on making a second trip to visit the homestead for a while, and until we can all sit down peaceably and discuss what we aim to do about Pa's legacy, I have too much time on my hands." He cracked a smile. "As Ma used to say, 'Idle hands make the devil's tools.'"

And some not so idle. The irritated recollection of Derek's recent thievery of the map rushed through Clay's mind. Regardless, the black fury that once roiled inside had tempered to weary bitterness. A week ago, Clay might have strongly objected to his brother including himself in on the events, unasked. He didn't anticipate spending more time than necessary in Derek's company, but strength grew in numbers. And Clay had no idea what they might find or if they might run across the outlaws responsible if those men returned to Meagan's former home for whatever reason. Illogical, but such men couldn't be called rational. Still, he couldn't deny Meagan her one request on the weakness of his speculation.

"So you have little doubt that the fire was no accident?" Clay directed his question to Kurt, ignoring Derek's not-so-subtle introduction of the mine, a subject he often brought up and Clay just as often avoided.

"The boy had been shot. Found him outside. I doubt his own ma shot him. Also, bein' as how she was trapped inside—barred in from the look of things—she would've never had a chance."

"Who would do such a despicable act?" Clay shook his head, disgusted.

"I have a hunch," Kurt admitted, "but don't want to say anything till I have more to go on."

Clay narrowed his eyes in disbelief. "Surely you don't think—"

"Meagan?" He finished Clay's question. "No. She's mighty peculiar, all right, claiming no recollection of what happened. But I doubt she's a cold-blooded killer with a heart so black she'd murder her own kin. She's much too distraught over what happened—what she can recall of it at any rate."

"Poor little gal." Derek's tone was sympathetic. "Left alone in the world and so young. Come to think of it, she must have kin elsewhere—didn't she mention a stepfather?" He directed his question to Clay.

Clay doubted a man like Landon McClinton cared about the family he'd left to struggle on their own and was surprised his brother would ask, owing to the personal history they shared. Unable to curb his mounting irritation, for the first time Clay addressed him. "She did, but I doubt he'd be concerned. You're right about one thing though—it is hard being left alone in the world without a soul to turn to or to care what happens. At least Meagan has us to help her through this. And I reckon a group of concerned strangers makes far better company than an estranged family member who puts his own desires first and lets his family suffer." As soon as the words left his mouth, Clay felt petty, wishing he could retrieve them, though he did nothing to make allowances for his jab.

From the wounded look in Derek's eyes, he got the message.

He rose from his chair. "Well, I reckon I've wasted enough time in the shade. I'd best see if Penny needs me. She has her hands full these days, and the girls have been a thorn in her side. This mining town is no place for them." He looked at Clay. "Once we find what we came for, I can take them home where they belong."

Clay refused to rise to the bait. "No one's stopping you."

"And I told you, I'm not searching unless you and Linda ride with me. That's the way Pa wanted it, and that's the way it's gonna stand."

Clay was surprised to hear Derek defend their excuse for a father. When they'd first reunited in Silverton, he'd been as disgusted with Pa as Clay had been. Now Derek spoke as if he'd forgotten all the old man had done to them. Before Clay could think of how to answer, Derek stepped off the boardwalk and strode toward his wagon.

"I know I haven't any right speaking on matters that don't concern me," Kurt said, watching Derek's back, "but I'm going to say my piece anyhow, since Linda's my wife and it concerns her. And I don't like seeing her unhappy." He shifted his attention to Clay. "I've known Derek going on a week, besides what little I saw of him when he came through Jasperville. He's a good man. Marshal Wilson wouldn't have befriended him had he not seen something admirable in his character. Sure, he's made his share of mistakes. He'd be the first to admit it and has told Linda and me what a selfish cuss he was, staying away while your ma was ill—"

Clay raised his hand for the deputy to stop. "I've heard all this—"

"What he hasn't told you," Kurt went on, deaf to Clay's words, "is that when he returned to Missouri after your ma died, he wanted to stay. But he didn't feel he had the right to ask or that you'd want him near. He did the best he knew how, and if you ask me, that's what counts when all is said and done."

Kurt moved to his feet, tugging the brim of his hat down to shade his eyes. "Truth is. . ." He looked at Derek, who Clay noticed had stopped in the street to greet a miner. The deputy shifted his gaze back to Clay. "I'd trust that man with my very life. And Linda's."

Lost in thought, Clay watched Kurt stride off after Derek. His brother seemed to have acquired an ability for easily gaining loyalty and friendships. Too bad he couldn't have shown the same respect and consideration toward his family.

Such sour thoughts once made Clay feel righteous in his resentment. Now they only made him feel. . .sour.

❧

Penny bustled through the curtain, a cheery smile spreading across her face when she saw Meagan awake and alert. "How are you this fine morning?"

Meagan didn't even try to smile. "My hands still ache something fierce."

"That's to be expected." Penny set down the clay bowl she carried. "Let's have a look then, shall we?"

Meagan held her breath as Penny unknotted and unwound the bandage from one of her hands. She had glimpsed them before when Penny tended her, but it had been enough to turn her stomach, and she'd averted her gaze every time after that. On this occasion, she forced herself to look. Now, as then, she grimaced at the shiny, rose-colored skin, save for sickly white blisters that had at least diminished in size and number. But the improvement amazed her. New skin had even started to grow in places.

"Praise the Lord for His mercy and goodness," Penny exclaimed, clearly pleased with the results. "Mind, you'll likely have scars, but you're mending nicely. Can you move your fingers?"

Meagan did so and winced. "They feel tight. Like the skin is stretched over bone."

"Don't look so sullen. 'Tis also a good sign of healing." Penny unwound the bandage of the other hand, then picked up the bowl, which contained the sticky paste she used for her poultices.

"And they itch something awful," Meagan added.

Penny laughed. "Another good sign."

"Just what is that?"

Penny seemed surprised by the question, since she'd used a concoction like it twice each day. But whereas Meagan never wanted details before, now her interest was piqued.

"A wee bit of herbs and extracts of plants my mother taught were good for such purposes. I don't know them by name, only by sight. Her mother taught her to use them—my Grandmother Kimama. She was of the Eastern Shoshone tribe. . . ." Penny continued to speak of her family as she spread the meal-like paste on a clean cloth and wrapped it around Meagan's hand. The warm poultice soothed her skin, and the itching eased. Meagan watched as Penny did the same to her other hand.

"There now," she exclaimed softly with a smile when she finished. "You'll be up and about in no time. How's your head feeling?" She leaned forward and applied gentle pressure to the lump, no longer as big as an egg. "It seems to be improving, as well."

"You're so good to me." Meagan's voice came quiet. "Why? I don't deserve such kindnesses."

Penny regarded her in surprise. "Whyever not? What have you done that's so terrible?"

Meagan shifted her gaze to the blanket.

"God doesn't want any of His children to suffer."

"You don't know what I've done."

"No matter. No sin lies beyond forgiveness."

Meagan only shook her head.

"Is this about what happened to you?"

She didn't answer. The memory may no longer exist, but her guilt lingered. How could she have left Ma and Wayne like that? After her talk with the deputy, a fleeting recollection had returned of walking through the wilds in her need to find help. Wayne had been sleeping, and she'd been unable to rouse him. . . . Something prickled in the back of her mind, something that urged her to remember. She shook her head, hoping the feeling would leave.

"There now," Penny soothed. "I think I know what you need to lift your spirits." With a mysterious smile, she retrieved the bowl and rose to her feet. "I'll be back shortly."

Alone, Meagan pondered her bleak situation, then thought of these people who'd done so much for her. Strangers—but they treated her like a cherished family member, spending time with her, taking care of her needs, even trying to make her smile. Something Meagan never thought possible until she spent time with Clay. He rarely spoke, but when he did, his words, whether trivial or significant, made Meagan feel good inside. Especially when he tried to be funny. After their first awkward moments, she enjoyed his company, as well as the children's. And their mother, Penny, was the kindest woman Meagan had ever met. It was only because of her Meagan had broken her silence. She couldn't abide listening to Penny suffer the brunt of blame the cruel man had tried to place on her for the fire, and only because her blood was part Indian.

Thoughts of the fire again took Meagan to that dreadful day. . . .

"No, stop it," she whispered, pressing her bandaged hands to her head. She couldn't let herself remember. . .so much lay in a haze she hoped never would resurface, because she didn't think she could bear the agony of knowing.

A razor-edged sliver of truth festered beneath her goose down layer of forgetfulness and hinted at something so terrible, she was certain it would make these good people despise her and want nothing more to do with her should they also learn the facts. She'd borne so much grief and didn't think she could endure Penny's disgust. Or Clay's rejection. Dwelling on tragic events would only bring her final ruination; she was sure of it. In disregarding what little she knew and never trying to recall those forgotten, shadowed areas lay her best course, and she feared returning to the site of her former home for that very reason. But her desire to bid her loved ones farewell and pay her last respects loomed more powerful than her fears. She owed them that much since she hadn't been there when they met their deaths. Or had she? No, she couldn't have been; she never would have walked away had she been in her right mind. Though after hearing two men talk outside the curtain's partition, she knew some in this hotel thought her crazy.

A persistent irritation jabbed at the forefront of her mind.

What if being there brings the memories back?

Meagan closed her eyes. She couldn't stay away; she just couldn't. If and when the time came, she would have to muster up strength to deal with the situation then.

Penny returned, Linda behind her, breaking Meagan from her relentless brooding. Both women bore bowls, containers, and cloths that made Meagan lift her brows in curious wonder.

The women smiled, and Meagan's heart gave a little jump of expectation.

six

"Clay, would you look in on Meagan?" Penny gave a sideways nod to the cubicle, her arms full of dirty linens. "I need to see to these."

Clay watched her swift retreat in surprise. Not that he minded spending time with Meagan; he often devised excuses for that very thing. But he thought it odd Penny would ask, odder still she would leave without awaiting his answer.

Meagan had long passed the critical stage and was slowly on the mend in body. As for her emotions, Clay suspected they were still in tatters and would remain that way for a while. Only time could heal deep wounds involved in the loss of loved ones and under such dreadful circumstances. He wished he could do something more for the plucky little sparrow, a term he'd begun to apply to her in his thoughts. Dirty, forlorn, and bedraggled, like a weak and helpless but brave little bird who'd flown through a bad storm. . . .

He stepped past the curtain and gaped, coming to a swift halt. His eyes soon stung from holding them wide in incredulity. Unblinking. Uncomprehending. . .

"Unbelievable."

He whispered the last to himself as he looked at the golden-haired angel in the blue-sprigged frock. Shyly, she regarded him. The black cinders and dirt washed from her hair, it shone dark golden, thick, and lush over her shoulders; the flame of an oil lamp caught glimmers of a lighter hue, like sprinklings of gold dust touching the strands. Her face scrubbed clean, the soft rose of her creamy skin heightened as he stared. But he couldn't help himself.

She broke eye contact and looked down at the blanket. Only then did Clay manage to force his gaze to something else. The flowers Christa brought. He wondered how they would look in Meagan's hair. The thought brought his wondering gaze back to her shining tresses.

Silence grew thick, and he knew he should speak. To gawk at her wasn't polite.

"You look better." He could have slapped himself at his gross understatement and lack of tact. His ma had taught him deportment and how to conduct himself in a lady's presence. "I mean, as if you're feeling better," he amended.

That didn't sound much improved—could he not have managed to pick and utter one of the many compliments revolving like a windmill through his head? He could have kissed her hand in homage to the princess, as Christa called her, when she offered him an understanding though still timid smile.

At the thought of giving her any kind of kiss, his face warmed.

"I, uh. . ." He scanned the confined room. Never before had it felt so small, and he scrambled in his mind for something to save him from the invisible noose that pulled tight around his neck. His eyes lit on the books sitting where he'd left them. He grabbed the top one of poetry. "Have you had a chance to thumb through this yet?" As soon as he asked, he remembered her condition and glanced at her bandaged hands.

Stupid, stupid. Of all the asinine remarks to make, that would range in the top few. . . .

"I was never taught how." She shrugged and smiled again.

Clay silently thanked her for disregarding his thoughtless question.

"Would you like me to read it? To you?" He tugged at his

collar, realizing he sounded like a callow youth who lacked the ability.

"Please." Her eyes sparkled with anticipation. At least she showed confidence in his skill, even if he felt as though his tongue might stick to the roof of his mouth if he tried. Why was it suddenly so dry?

The poppy blue in her dress brought out the golden flecks in her eyes. Her dark lashes made them glow even brighter.

He decided he needed a dipper of water first and felt grateful Penny had left a container behind.

"That's remarkable that you know your letters," Meagan said as he drank. "I never met a man who could read. Except you. And your friends."

"Uh, yeah." He didn't sound as if he could string two decent words together, let alone read them. "My ma was a schoolmarm back East. When she lived there." *Of course when she lived there—when else?* Now if he could just get other things to work right, like his brain.

Clay took a seat on the ground, wondering if he sat too close. She leaned forward in anticipation. "I never had anyone read to me before. Ma didn't know her letters well, even if we'd had books to read. She tried to teach me what she did know, but there wasn't time. Always too much work to do." A waft of her fresh scent rushed over him, reminding him of a sweet meadow of spring flowers.

Much too close.

He scooted back as far as the canvas wall allowed and noted the curious tilt of her head. He'd sensed her attractive features beneath the layers of soot, but he'd never taken her for a beauty. The most beautiful woman he'd ever seen. . . He swallowed over the fast-growing lump in his throat and flipped the book open at random.

Read, he commanded himself.

He cleared his throat and began, " 'So far as our story approaches the end, which do you pity the most of us three? My friend, or the mistress of my friend with her wanton eyes, or me. . . ?' "

The heat building inside burned through his face and over his ears. "Uh, let's try another one. That poem sounds like it began earlier in the book, though I started with the first line, but I'm sure I can find something more suited to the occasion." He flipped pages, figuring the second title that caught his eye—"The Englishman in Italy"—would give no further embarrassment.

" '*Piano di Sor-rento*,' " he stumbled over the foreign words, " '*For-tù, Fortù,* my beloved one, sit here by my side. . .on my knees. . .put up both little feet—' " His last words came out a bare rasp.

He flipped the pages again, in danger of tearing them as he pushed them aside, as if the printed words might somehow take a mind of their own and rise from the pages, blaring out their unseemly messages. The heat crawled to the back of his neck. "Time's Revenge" sounded far safer and much more distant. He heaved a calming breath and again cleared his throat. " 'I've a Friend, over the sea; I like him, but he loves me. . .' "

He slammed the book shut, noting the author, Robert Browning, and promising himself that Penny would pay for her little joke on him. *Dramatic Lyrics* was the misleading title the book had been given. A "book of poems," his sweetly conniving sister-in-law had said—more like a book of love sonnets! He'd read poetry—before he went to live in Mr. Dougherty's storeroom. Old Lady Harper had a shelf of books he'd "borrowed" when he was sure he could take one without her knowledge in between the many chores she allotted him—but that book of poetry that had appealed to his boyish senses and told of a horseman's ghostly ride held nothing like what this book contained.

Clay didn't dare look at Meagan. The words he'd read lingered in the air, taking on an uncomfortable association with the woman who sat so vulnerable and trusting at his side. They wove a closeness that made him all too conscious of the scant distance separating them. Every whisper of movement she made, her sweet scent enticing, her long fall of silken hair tempting his touch. . .

Afraid his hands might actually betray his thoughts, he clasped the book tighter. If it were made of glass, it might have cracked in his desperate grip.

Silence crept on uneasy toes between them but seemed to snicker behind its shielded mouth at Clay.

"That was Penny's book," he said in apology. "I'd never read it before now and had no idea. . . ." His words trailed off.

"What about the other book?" Her voice also sounded hoarse. "Would you read that one to me?"

"Uh, I suppose." Clay withheld a groan, wondering if Penny had left behind the first book she'd offered as part of a plan, knowing this might happen. At least that book wouldn't make his insides crawl or shock his listener with prose that felt far too familiar, as if the intimate words applied to Meagan and himself and not two fictional characters the writer had fabricated. He'd heard the message of the other book before, so he knew there would be no undesirable surprises. That was the most he could say for reading it.

With a sigh, he picked up the huge volume Penny had wrapped in cloth, unwound it, and laid it on his lap. He opened to the first page.

" 'In the beginning God created the heaven and the earth. And the earth was without form, and void; and darkness was upon the face of the deep. And the Spirit of God moved upon the face of the waters. . . .'"

Feeling calmer, Clay settled into a more comfortable position and continued to read aloud.

≥&

"How are you feeling? You sure you're ready for this?"

Meagan smiled at the almost constant consideration Clay showed her.

"I'm much better," she assured for what seemed the hundredth time that morning. "I'll sit inside and won't do any walking till we get there."

He rested his hand at her elbow even before they reached the wagon and sent her insides all topsy-turvy again. But this new sensation that came with frequency the past week and a half had nothing to do with the fast-diminishing lump on her head. She had recovered to the point that she'd left the bed and had taken to joining the Burke family at their meals. This was her first outing.

"Something paining you?" Clay asked in concern. He looked down at her hands, wound in bandages, though not so thickly as before.

She hadn't realized he watched her every expression and had seen her wince. "I was thinking how last time I took a journey it was months by wagon with Ma and Pa."

"You never did mention what happened to him."

Meagan smiled sadly. "His health was always poor. We hoped moving west would change that, but he died on the journey. That was near two years back. . .and now settlers will be coming all the way from the east by locomotive, their journey taking less than a week. It just doesn't seem possible, does it?"

Meagan looked past the small, bustling town and snow-topped mountains eastward, as if she could already see the column of smoke from a distant locomotive. What would it be like to travel by such means? Would she ever get the opportunity? She couldn't imagine riding through wide barren plains without feeling the scorching rays from the sun, or traveling so high in the pine-laden mountains, without freezing from sudden snowstorms or getting dizzy. How wonderful to ride through the West by railroad and suffer no ill effects, only to sit and look at the beauty of the land laid out all around her. . . .

"Any time you're ready, I think they're waiting on us," Clay urged, his voice quiet. Tenderness misted his eyes, making her heart beat a little faster. Their color was the clear blue of a mountain lake, and the manner in which he looked at her made her feel light-headed—despite their low altitude or the lack of a lump on her noggin.

Her mouth too dry to speak, she nodded, and they walked to the wagon. The two couples and children smiled at their approach.

Penny had insisted she come along, since some of the seeds and plants she used, both for remedies and her beautiful pouches, grew near the river. At supper the previous night, she'd assured her husband, who opposed the idea because of "possible danger," that she could handle a firearm as well as any man—and hadn't she proven so when they first met? At her claim, Derek had grinned, and they shared a private look Meagan had since wondered about.

Whereas Derek would prefer his wife remain behind, Kurt wouldn't hear of such a notion with regard to Linda. The spirited redhead offered to stay in the hotel with the children, but Kurt refused, and Meagan assumed he feared for her security. She knew something of their past through supper conversation, including Linda's recent abduction by a crooked sheriff from her hometown. Two outlaw brothers, wanted dead or alive, had worked for him and his cohort. Kurt wanted to take no chances with Linda's safety should the pair of outlaws arrive in Silverton.

Meagan had asked Clay to come, wanting his support more than all the others, so it turned out all of the Burke clan, their spouses, and the children would accompany Meagan. Penny and Linda had even packed a picnic for the occasion, thanks to Jinx's generosity in giving them supplies from his kitchen.

Still unable to use her wrapped hands without difficulty— Penny insisted the bandages stay on, her condition for this trip—Meagan pondered how to climb into the wagon bed. She stood alone at the rear, the others having congregated to the front and sides, talking in groups. She heard the scuff of shoes in the dirt as someone approached from behind. "Need some help?" Clay's deep voice came to her, and before she knew what was happening, he swept her up into his strong arms.

Her heart beating as fast as the chirps of a nearby bird, she blinked up into his shuttered eyes, only inches from her own, and held her breath. His heart raced just as fast beneath her arm trapped against his chest. Yet before she could wonder if he might actually kiss her—and, oh how her head swam at the sweet thought—he gently deposited her in the back of the wagon.

She could barely think, much less frame words to thank him. He tipped his hat and grinned before striding away, sending her heart, much battered from all its rapid drumming, straight into her stomach. Or so it felt. What was wrong with her?

She'd seen Clay every day for more than a week. Going on two. When she was laid up, he'd visited and they talked. He'd read to her from the Good Book, which so intrigued Meagan, she had asked him to read from it whenever they were together. But here she sat, acting as if she'd never seen the man. No, that wasn't exactly right. . .more to the point, acting as if she'd like to see much more of him. Alone. To sit by his side and put her little feet upon his knees, as in the poem he'd read. . . .

Livvie and Christa appeared, breaking into Meagan's wistful thinking. They climbed in the back, chattering about their upcoming adventure. Face warm, Meagan forced her mind to abandon the dangerous territory of Clayton Burke and focus instead on the girls. Christa held a doll with a cloth face and black seeds sewn for eyes and nose, red ones for a mouth.

"Is that your doll?" Meagan asked, smiling at the child.

Christa nodded. "I had another, but it got ruint, so Mama made this one for my birthday." She hugged the rag doll close, and Meagan noticed its dress matched Christa's red calico. She thought of her own doll, "ruint" when Wayne, as a tot, used to gnaw on it and bit off one of its button eyes. She, at five years old, had slugged him when she saw Jane dangling from his mouth, but not hard enough to hurt, though he'd squalled as if she did. The recollection brought a bittersweet jab to her heart. She and Wayne fought, like all brothers and sisters, but they had their good times, too. Now she only had memories.

"Dolls are for babies," Livvie staunchly remarked.

Meagan noted Christa's downcast eyes as she hugged her doll closer.

"I know how special they are," she told Christa. "I had a doll once. Had her till I was nine years old, if I remember right." She chuckled. "Truth is, I can't remember when I stopped carrying her with me."

Her words brought back Christa's radiant smile. Livvie only grunted.

Linda climbed inside, and Kurt followed, resting a rifle over his legs. Meagan hoped his defensive act was ingrained, that of a lawman's routine, and not a sign that he expected trouble.

He caught her glance at the weapon and gave a reassuring smile.

With everyone packed inside, the space grew cramped. Penny sat beside her husband, who drove the wagon, and Clay rode behind on horseback. As they traveled, from time to time, Meagan glimpsed his fine form through the gap in the canvas tarpaulin that covered the wagon bed. . .the creaks and rattles of the wagon soon became natural, and the dreaming of which her ma so often accused her once more took wing in Meagan's heart.

What would it be like to sit beside him in the shade, away from all eyes, with his arm around her shoulders? Or perhaps near a glowing hearth as he read to her from that poetry book, those words becoming theirs. . .to run her fingers along his strong jaw and feel his lips brush against hers? Cool as refreshing water or warm as the morning sun? She pondered what it might feel like to kiss Clay, to belong to him completely, as Penny belonged to Derek and Linda to Kurt. She would pass her eighteenth year come July, already past the conventional age of marrying, according to her ma, who'd wed Meagan's pa at sixteen. . . .

"So, tell us, Meagan, how did you come to live in the wilds?" The abrupt question probed into her pleasant daydream.

Linda's eyes regarded her with friendship, nothing cruel or superior about them. Meagan was sure by now these good people were rife with curiosity regarding her history and couldn't begrudge their interest. But she was extremely grateful Linda couldn't read her mind! She might think she *was* a woman from the wilds, or more to the point, a wild woman with little sense.

"When we left the wagon train, Ma met Landon McClinton. He was panning for gold. She didn't have enough provisions to feed us and couldn't continue to Oregon, so she married him and settled here. He made his home where he searched and found enough gold dust to scrape out a living. Last month, he left for Carson City when he got wind that a former partner who'd robbed him was staying there. . . . Landon left us behind to guard the land from claim jumpers." Her last words came slow as the reason why her stepfather left resurfaced without trouble, when before it had been lost beyond the dark curtains that clouded her memory.

"Claim jumpers?" Linda and Kurt shared an alarmed glance, which made Meagan wonder, but she felt more anxious with her own predicament than curious over theirs.

Were those bleak moments lost to her coming back? If so, she might remember all that happened, and she wasn't certain she could bear it. The dread that she might somehow have been responsible for her family's demise ate away at her newly acquired calm. If outsiders had done it, why had they spared her? Why were her hands so badly burned, but, save for the lump on her head, the rest of her body suffered only minor injuries?

"I think Whisper would be a nice name, bein' as how Princess Rose won't work." Christa's voice broke the quiet.

"Whisper's a stupid name." Livvie rolled her eyes. "Whoever heard of a horse called Whisper?"

"Uncle Clay's horse makes a whispery sound when it whickers."

"All horses do that."

"Uncle Clay's horse does it even more," Christa argued with a pout.

"I think what you girls need is some fresh air and sunshine," Linda broke in, likely an effort to bring peace before yet another skirmish arose between sisters.

"Aye," Christa said, acting more grown up than her years and hugging her doll close. "Ruby and I want to pick flowers."

"Ruby is your doll's name?" Meagan asked, grateful for her mind's reprieve. "That's pretty. Rubies are rare jewels. I've never seen one, but I hear they're dark red in color like your dresses."

Christa beamed at her.

"I wanna go outside. My legs are all cramped up stiff from sitting like this." Livvie approved Linda's suggestion, though her words came out as a complaint.

"Derek," Linda called up. "The girls want to walk."

The wagon rolled to a stop, and the two crawled out, eager to explore the land as they followed along. If Meagan felt able, she would have joined them. She'd always preferred the wide outdoors to a stuffy room, and trapped behind tarpaulin, she could see little of the broad, sagebrush plain.

"Are you feeling all right?" Linda's mouth drew down in concern.

Meagan didn't feel well at all but assured Linda she was. What ailed her couldn't be treated with rest in bed and poultices.

seven

"You two get restless already?" Clay greeted the girls as they scampered through the scrub and short grass toward him. "It hasn't even been an hour."

"Can I ride?" Christa greeted, her dark eyes shining as she tilted her head all the way up to see his face.

"I thought you wanted to pick flowers," Livvie said.

"Right now I want to ride with Uncle Clay." Christa raised her arms high to be picked up.

Sensing the friction between the two, Clay wrapped his reins around the pommel.

"All right, sweet potato, get on up here." While holding the saddle with one hand, he leaned down, wrapped an arm under both of Christa's as she clung to his shoulder the best she could while holding her doll, and hoisted her up in front of him. She weighed so little, and he recalled Penny's concern when she and Derek first arrived in Silverton. Christa had been sickly but with rest had soon recovered, though she still looked young for her scant years and weighed little more than his bedroll.

"Now then, what's wrong?" he asked once they were under-way and following the wagon.

"I don't like Livvie," Christa complained. "She's mean. She never used to be thatta way, not before we moved to Silverton and she started spending time with Jinx and Tucker. I like them, but it seems she's always in their company. And she's always bossin' me around and tellin' me what to do like Tucker does Jinx."

Clay recalled Penny's qualms that her girls might pick up the poor habits of the miners they lived among and watched every day. Too bad they didn't spend more time in Gentleman George's company. Not only would their speech come out proper, they might learn a manner or two.

"I imagine you'll be friends again soon," he soothed, though he had no idea how to counsel his niece. Mrs. Harper and Mr. Dougherty both had small children, but Clay had never been accepted as a member of either family, treated more as a servant without a logical thought of his own. Not that he minded Mr. Dougherty's gruff instructions, since he considered himself as making his own living there, but in Old Lady Harper's household, her frequent condescension and slights against "that dreadful orphan boy" had stung more than he'd let on.

He'd never had much of a true family and desired to say and do the right thing by his niece, aside from the fact that should he fail in his duties as an uncle and lead Christa astray, he might expose himself to a dose of Penny's motherly wrath. And lately, she'd been acting more than a little strange.

"Livvie doesn't wanna be my friend no more," Christa insisted. "Not ever. She doesn't like nothin' about me."

"That can hurt," Clay commiserated. "But you mustn't let her hateful words get the best of you, 'cause they can squeeze all the happiness clean out your middle—and then where would you be?" He tightened his arm around her midsection in a squeeze of mock admonishment, and she giggled. "All tight and hard and cross, that's where. You've gotta learn to rise above others' taunts, Christa, be satisfied with who you are. If Livvie doesn't like you, I reckon that's her problem, not yours. Just ignore her. Eventually she'll get to wondering why you're not bothered any longer and might even want to make peace when she sees her taunts don't affect you as they once did."

Christa craned her head around as far as it would go to look at him. "Is that what you and Pa did when you were young?" Her earnest eyes shone up at him.

He grinned at the idea that she considered twenty old, but her innocent question brought to mind his boyhood squabbles with Derek, usually rectified by sundown. A nostalgic pang stung him, and he wished things could go back to what they once were, then felt surprised at his change of heart. The situation as it stood wasn't Clay's fault, despite Penny's and Linda's gentle rebukes to make him feel otherwise. Derek had created the breach by stealing the maps. Clay had every right to be cross and not trust his brother.

Christa returned her gaze to the wagon, sparing Clay the need to reply.

"I don't care if she likes Ruby or not. Miss Meagan likes her. And Miss Meagan's nice. Pretty, too, like a princess in one of Grandda's tales. You think she's pretty, Uncle Clay?"

His awkwardness advanced to a loftier height. "Uh, sure."

"I asked Mama if she could come live with us and be my sister, bein' as how she hasn't got family no more. But Mama said she'll likely wanna start her own, since she's a woman and not a child." She craned her head to look up at him again. "I think you should marry her, Uncle Clay. Then we can keep her with us forever."

Her earnest remark so staggered Clay he nearly let go of the reins. He tightened his grip as the leather strips burned through his fingers, adjusting his hold before he lost all control and his horse took the bit and galloped off. Much as their innocent conversation about sibling rivalry had done.

With a keen sort of desperation, he hoped Christa would drift to another subject, as she was apt to do, or run out of steam for the current one and grow silent.

"Please? Say you will. I don't want her going away when

her hands get better and she doesn't need us to wait on her no more." She blinked up at him, clearly expecting an answer.

"Christa, I can't marry her." He scrambled for a suitable reply. When she didn't look satisfied he added, "Such matters aren't even discussed till after the courting is done."

"What's courtin'?"

Beneath his hat, his ears burned in his discomfort. "I never courted a woman, but I hear it's when two people take a liking to each other and spend time in one another's company."

"You've been spending time with her and reading to her," she said with childish wisdom so lacking in adult sense.

"Well. . .yes." His face grew uncomfortably hot, having little to do with the great ball of sun blazing overhead. Her innocent remark brought to mind the not-so-innocent book of poetry.

"Don't you like her enough to marry her?"

"Sure I do. I mean, no, I can't." He felt as flustered as a boy who knew nothing of love, not that he claimed to know much at all.

"She likes you. I can tell."

He managed to swallow over the lump in his throat. "A person can like another person without wanting to marry them, Christa."

"So you don't wanna marry her?"

How did the conversation lose all semblance of control and speed downhill so fast? He looked ahead to the wagon, hoping Penny might call for her girls, that the wagon might stop for a rest break, that Livvie might backtrack with a question—anything to save him from this current predicament. But no such luck. The wagon plodded on, its occupants not calling out any orders, while Livvie kicked something aside with her foot and bent to collect what Clay assumed was ammunition for her slingshot—not running back with any questions.

He had dug himself into this pit, handing Christa the shovel with which to bury him. Now he had to find a way out before he choked. The neckline of his shirt came low, but his throat was tight; he couldn't seem to draw enough air into his lungs.

"Matters of marriage should be discussed between the two who plan on doing the marrying. Not among outsiders, especially not small children."

His serious explanation triggered the opposite reaction than what he'd desired.

"Then you *do* like Miss Meagan and wanna marry her!" she exclaimed with a smile as big as Christmas.

"No, I didn't say that," he hastily amended. "Only that when and if the time ever comes to talk over the matter, it should be done in private, and only between me and the woman I'm courting." Just saying the words made him uneasy. His hands felt clammy. "But I've got far too much to take care of before I look into finding a wife and settling down."

"You mean the silver mine," she said matter-of-factly, and he sent a sharp glance her way.

"You know about that?"

"Me and Livvie heard Mama and Pa talk when they was alone."

"Seems to me you two eavesdrop a lot more than you should." He spoke with a sense of relief that the conversation had veered to another course. Upon hearing his words, he worried she might get the wrong impression and tried again. "You shouldn't eavesdrop at all. It isn't polite."

"I just did it 'cause Livvie did."

"Like you followed her to the dance hall the other day?"

Christa looked stricken with worry. "You know about that?" she whispered.

"Beulah told me. A woman who works there. I saw her in

the tin shop," he hurriedly added. He didn't want his niece to think he'd visited an old pastime and taken to the drink again. She might tell Penny, and, misconception or not, he'd never hear the end of it. In fact, the old temptation hadn't revisited once since he'd found Meagan.

"Mama would take a switch to our backsides if she knew. I just went 'cause Livvie called me 'a lily-livered baby coward' when I said Mama wouldn't like it. We didn't go inside, just looked through the slats in the doors." She sucked in her lower lip. "You won't tell?"

Clay considered her plea. "Only if you promise never to go there again. It's not a place for little girls. Especially good little girls, like your mama is raising you to be."

She nodded in an exaggerated motion. "I won't be bad no more."

"That's good to know. But if you break your word, I'll tell. Promises work both ways."

After solemnly swearing she would stay far from the dance hall, she grew quiet. Clay felt thankful for the stretch of peace and especially that she'd forgotten her childish matchmaking ploys. The last thing he needed was a wife. He had no income, no homestead—certainly no way to provide. Regardless, Christa's words pecked at him like a hen's sharp beak. No matter how he tried, he couldn't erase their association to Meagan from his mind.

Soon Christa wanted down, and Clay brought his horse to a halt. Her glossy dark braids bounced near her waist as she sprinted through small clumps of sagebrush to catch up to Livvie, her animosity toward her sister evidently forgotten. As Clay watched the two walk together, he pondered what a child of Meagan's might look like. Bright yellow hair, golden green eyes, and a smile as potent as sunshine after a long rain. . .

He caught himself and shook his head to clear it. Riding

in the hot sun all morning had muddled his thinking. His thoughts sure didn't need to inhabit such trails.

At noon, they stopped to eat half of what the women had packed. Clay felt grateful for the strips of meat between slabs of mesquite bread. After a daily diet of Jinx's stews, the women's labors in the kitchen came as a treat, and they'd made enough to feed a small army. In retrospect, he figured that's what they were.

He sat apart from the others, knowing he wouldn't make good company at the moment, but when Meagan came near, he didn't suggest she join the women. Nor did he offer much by way of conversation. Christa's promptings of marriage whined inside his head, and he couldn't help but notice Meagan's confused glances in his direction.

Once they were underway again, Clay relaxed, then grew alert as they approached the area where he'd first found Meagan. Any moment, they should arrive at the gravesite, since Kurt mentioned he hadn't buried her family far from their home.

The wagon continued plodding forward. At each minute that elapsed, Clay's amazement increased. He realized how full of pluck Meagan was to have covered such an expanse of ground on foot and in her condition. She was a remarkable girl in every sense of the word, and if Clay had something more than himself to offer, he would take Christa's words to heart. Once he found Pa's mine, maybe then he could consider the prospect—at least tell Meagan how he felt. And he did feel something for her, deep and true and dear, but he certainly wouldn't admit that to his six-year-old niece.

The wagon rolled to a stop after about an hour. Clay looked around him. Nothing but flat scrubland and low hills. Then he noticed it far up ahead. What remained of a small shack stood before a hill. Much of the roof had caved in, and what rocks formed the walls had blackened. A gap stood where a door had been. The entire place looked in danger of collapsing. He wondered what marvel of gravity kept it upright.

Slowly they piled from the wagon, and Clay watched for Meagan. Once she emerged with Kurt's help, he dismounted, his gaze never leaving her slight form. She remained silent as Kurt pointed toward two mounds of dirt. Rocks in the shape of a cross were piled over each one. With hesitant steps, she approached and stood at the site where her loved ones lay buried. Her shoulders bowed, and her head hung low.

Clay wanted nothing more than to go to her but felt she needed time alone. Not once though, did he take his eyes off her small form.

⁂

"Ma, I'm so sorry," Meagan whispered, the guilt overwhelming and pressing in as she dropped to her knees. "If I'd been where I should have, maybe none of this would've ever happened." The details were still sketchy, but since arriving at what remained of her home, bits and pieces grew clearer.

She'd been foolish to come but couldn't pass up the opportunity of being close to her family one last time, to pay her respects. Her gaze shifted to the second mound of dirt, shorter than the first, and her fingertips pressed gently into the fine grains. "Wayne, I'm sorry I yelled at you for cracking the eggs. You couldn't help being clumsy. Seems we fought every day, but I still loved you. I loved you both."

Shadows moved across the land, and she glanced at the sky. Gray-rimmed clouds swept over the sun. . . . She wrinkled her brow as a memory tried to surface.

"I just wanted you to know that," she whispered quickly and stood, brushing the soil from her skirt. She felt Clay's presence behind her, giving much-needed support.

He laid his hand against her upper arm. "The others have

gathered at the river."

His words reminded her of the song Derek had told her they'd sung here, giving her some comfort. She nodded that she was ready, and Clay helped her walk the short distance, his arm supporting her shoulders as though afraid she might stumble or fall. The sky had darkened a shade, close to the color of ashes, and a picture of another day flashed across her mind. She abruptly stopped walking.

"Meagan?" Clay asked in concern.

She closed her eyes, and the picture faded. "I'm all right." Her voice came hoarse, proving her words a lie.

"If you'd rather go back to the wagon. . ."

"No." She straightened her back. "I want to join the others." If she concentrated on other things when the pictures flashed through her mind, she could do this. She'd sat inside the stuffy wagon half the day and could scarce tolerate the thought of returning to its confines.

Once they came to the river near the rocks where she and Wayne had scouted in their own childlike quest for precious ores, Meagan noticed that Penny and Linda sat there with the girls, quietly talking.

Upon seeing her approach, Christa slowly rose and just as slowly walked toward her. "I'm sorry 'bout your mama," she whispered, uncertain. She held out her doll. "Would you like to hold Ruby? It made me feel better to hold my doll after my first papa died from a snake bite."

Touched by the sweet gesture, Meagan offered the child the best smile she could muster under the circumstances and took the rag doll. It did help to hold on to something. She stood at the river and stared into the water. Another glimpse of that awful day rushed through her head, a moment she'd forgotten.

Flashes of light and shadow. The dour laughter of men.

She shut her eyes.

"Meagan?" Clay asked in alarm. "You've gone white as a ghost! What's wrong?" He took hold of her arm as though worried she might fall. "You're remembering, aren't you?"

She didn't respond, only looked westward along the river's course. The clouds overhead blocked out the sun and resembled the way the region had looked that day. As though a force greater than her strong will propelled her, she moved trancelike along the riverbank, slowly breaking from Clay's hold while she clutched the doll to her bosom. Flashes brought further images to mind. Once more, she halted her steps and shut her eyes tight, willing the images away. . . .

This time they didn't fade.

❧

Ma would be angry. Nothing but a dreamer, she called Meagan, and Meagan supposed Ma was right to feel that way. She should have been home ages ago, but the way the sunlight danced along the surface of the river made Meagan forget her chore of collecting the water. Instead she watched it glisten and move as though it were a living thing. The beads of golden light jumped along the slow-moving river, entrancing her, and she wondered about life beneath its sparkling surface, about the fish that swam there. What would the light look like from beneath? Just as bright and dazzling or mysterious and ghostly? She wished she could find out.

The golden nuggets of light disappeared from the ribbon of brown water, and she looked up, puzzled. A thick veil of storm clouds had pushed across the glowing face of the sun. Regardless, she doubted it would rain; the land seldom received any.

"Well, now, what have we here?" a man's drawl from behind sent a bevy of instant chills popping along her arms.

She jumped up in shock, upsetting the empty wooden bucket and knocking it into the river. The current tugged it toward the middle. Before she could grab the container, the man closest to her clamped his huge hand around her arm.

"My brother and I are thirsty. Fetch us a drink, girl."

"M–my bucket." Woefully, she stared at the bucket, now yards away in the deeper water, then at him. "It's too far out."

"Then you best go get it!" He gave her a push that sent her falling on her hands and knees. Water splashed into her mouth and nose, making her cough and choke. The men's evil laughter churned her stomach in knots of fear.

"Please. . ." She tried to rise, but her knees shook so badly, she fell down again. The current pulled at her dress, increasing her panic. "I can't swim!"

The man grabbed her by the arm again, pulling her from the water and to him like a spineless rag doll. Holding her tight and dripping against him, his chest and arms were as solid as the nearby rocks, his manner as ruthless. Tears burned down her cheeks. "Let me go! What do you want with me?"

"Well now," he leered, studying her sodden form. "I can think of a good many things. What do you say, Amos? Shall we have some fun?"

She struggled to escape, but his grip was too strong, her wet skirts too heavy. Suddenly, he sent her sailing from him with a push. The other man caught her from behind, his arms wrapping like steel rods around her middle. His fetid breath made her feel she might heave as he whispered near her ear, "She's a beauty, all right. And we got nothin' else to do till we find them maps." He nipped her lobe hard, chuckling when she yelped in pained revulsion, then tossed her back into his brother's arms. The first man held her the same as before, his hand taking liberties that shocked her virginal mind and summoned her fighting spirit from hibernation.

"No! You won't touch me, you lechers!" She fought and

kicked and scratched, making it difficult for him to keep his hold on her. The other man tried to grab her legs, but she kicked him hard in the face with the heel of her shoe. He groaned, backing up and holding his nose. Blood poured from both nostrils. The sight gave her added courage that she *could* escape, and she twisted her upper body, bringing back her elbow fast, and knocked her evil captor hard in the jaw. He lessened his hold on her with an oath, and she scratched at his eyes.

That won her complete freedom. She darted away, bending down to pick up a fist-sized rock while facing them off. "Either of you come one step nearer, and I'll bash your brains in, so help me." She tried to appear brave and strong, though salty tears fell without control, leaking into her mouth. Backing up, she raised the rock high in continued threat, then spun around.

Hampered by her sodden skirts, she fled as fast as she could in the opposite direction from home, finding refuge in a shallow cave she and Wayne had discovered weeks before. There, she hid within its dark recesses, her arms tight around her knees as she shivered, the dank air chilling, while she kept her ears attuned to the least little sound. Some time passed before she gathered enough courage to leave. Slow and careful, she trekked home, keeping watch for the men, the rock ready in her hand. She had never let it go.

The pungent odor of smoke alarmed her as she took the bend of the hill leading home. In horror she saw what had been their shack, flames from the inside shooting from the sod and stone, up toward the darkened sky. Wayne lay facedown on the ground near one wall, the fire not yet reaching him.

"Wayne!" she raced to him, stumbling on legs that felt like jelly, and pulled at his shoulders to rouse him. "Wake up! Hurry! The house is on fire!"

Terrified and confused, she noticed the door, barred from the outside. Fire licked through its planks. She gave up trying to rouse her brother and tried to lift the bar, pounding at the flames with her bare hands, to no avail. Her palms throbbed in agony as the flames seared her flesh; the foul black smoke made her choke. Nevertheless, she persisted, screaming for her ma, screaming for help from heaven above until her throat felt as raw as her hands and her pleas became ragged croaks. Something from above—likely a rock—broke from the wall and hit her skull.

Next thing she remembered, she woke up with a throbbing headache, coughing as her throat tickled and burned. She turned part of her face out of the mud and blinked up at the sky from where she lay on the ground, as sodden as she. The fire had petered out; the sound of rainwater an almost comforting splash as it poured from what remained of the roof to puddle on the ground. In places, small patches of fire still burned low, but all was too wet to give the flames added fuel.

"Ma?"

No answering sound came from inside the cabin. Worse, Meagan could recall nothing of what happened or how she'd ended up flat on the ground in a seldom-received rainstorm. It had all seemed like a strange nightmare with no beginning. . . .

❧

Meagan kept her eyes shut as slow tears dripped down her cheeks to run off her jaw. Clay's hand on her shoulder gave her the strength needed to recall the rest of that day. She had remembered the worst; she must recall the rest.

She had managed to rise from the mud, her hands throbbing with fierce pain, her sole aim to find help from somewhere, all the while wondering where her ma had gone, her mind blocking out the truth. She kept calling for her ma as her brother lay still. In her shock, she'd been sure he only slept or figured he'd been conked on the head, too. She recalled Landon's talk of miners with a claim to the west. Trancelike, she'd staggered from the remnants of her home without a second glance at Wayne, hoping her ma would soon return from wherever she'd gone and rouse him.

The sky had still loomed overcast from the sudden squall. With no sun to guide her and her mind so muddled that the hills crowding the area all looked alike, she had walked east instead of west until Clay found her. Looking back on it now, she felt surprised she'd gotten so far. Penny once told her the Almighty led her to Clay, and Clay to her. But why should someone as powerful and great as the Almighty God whom Clay had read about save such a wicked girl as herself? The truth she had dreaded became clear—she had been partially to blame for her family's deaths.

Once she'd awakened in Silverton, even the memory of her need to find help had abandoned her, along with the other bleak and frightening recollections that the curtain of blankness concealed. But now she remembered all she'd forgotten.

Contrary to the breakdown she'd expected, a strength she never anticipated gave Meagan new resolve. She turned eyes still wet with tears to Clay, her mouth fixed in a grim line. She would not cry, not again.

Linda approached, cautious, and Meagan looked from Clay to his sister. "Tell your husband I recall all of what happened and have the information he needs to catch those men. They killed my family. I want them brought to justice."

Linda wrapped her arm around Meagan's shoulders. "I'll come with you."

"I'll come, too," Clay said as Linda moved with Meagan in the direction of the wagon. He took only a few steps before Linda turned.

"Best stay with Penny, Clay. I think she has something she'd like to discuss with you." Her words sounded almost apologetic.

"She's right, I do need to speak with you," his sister-in-law said from behind.

He didn't bother hiding his impatience. "It can't wait?"

"No. It cannot." Penny looked just as determined.

eight

Clay sighed, watching Meagan walk away, then turned to Penny. "If this is another method of yours to get me alone to harp on me about Derek. . ."

Her mouth pulled into a thin line. "No, but it does concern him."

"Penny," he warned.

"He and I discussed the matter on the ride here, and we think it would be a grand idea to stay overnight. Linda's agreeable; I spoke with her earlier. She wants to talk to Kurt, but I can't see that he would refuse."

Clay regarded her with some surprise. "Don't you think staying in this area where her loved ones were murdered might be difficult for Meagan after all she's been through?"

She drew her brows together in concern. "Aye, it would. I'd never dream of causing her such grief. I intend to speak with Derek about moving upriver. There's enough daylight remaining to put some distance behind us."

Clay blew out a frustrated breath. "And just why is this so important?"

"It will give us opportunity to discuss the mine freely without fear of being overheard."

"What about Meagan?"

"Neither Derek nor myself nor Linda think she's a concern. Do you?"

He didn't but wouldn't give in that easily. "Like I told Derek, I'm not interested in discussing the mine."

"Well now, you're not the only Burke alive!" Her eyes

flashed, but her voice remained calm. "Whatever you decide, whether you'll be joining us or not, is entirely up to you. The rest of us wish to discuss the matter before the days become too hot to search." She turned with a whirl of her skirts.

"Penny—wait!"

She stopped her swift retreat and looked over her shoulder.

"A question." He kept his voice moderate. "Were you really wanting my vote or hoping for my compliance?"

"Both, of course."

He snorted. "Fair enough. I can give you one—I don't mind staying the night. But not the other. I have no intention of discussing the mine." He only spoke the truth of his feelings; so why did he feel like such an ingrate? She had a way of doing that to him, and he hated it. It made him feel much younger to her than the seven or so years that separated them.

"About what I expected. Now if you'll be excusing me, I need to see to dinner."

"One more moment of your time?"

"Aye?" The word seethed with frustration. She halted but didn't turn to him, offering only a partial view of her face.

"About that book of poetry. . ."

He thought he saw her mouth flicker in a smile.

"That was a cruel move, Penny. I'm sure it embarrassed Meagan as much as it did myself."

"You read it to her, then?"

"Till I couldn't stand to read any more."

"Well now, Clay." This time she pivoted all the way around to face him. "It was your choice to read it. I dinnae twist your arm. I offered another book first, a much better one, but you refused. So doona be parceling out blame where blame's not due. I'm not a walking library."

Pulling his mouth in a scowl, as upset as she, Clay looked away and stared at the slow-moving water.

Penny offered Meagan a sandwich, but she shook her head. She didn't think her stomach could tolerate food.

Sitting at the edge of the wagon, their legs and skirts dangling nearly to the ground, both women stared toward the sun, almost a memory now as twilight closed in and the clouds cresting the hills turned violet.

"You must eat," Penny urged. "You cannot starve yourself in punishment that you don't even deserve."

"If I hadn't hidden in that cave and instead had warned them, Ma and Wayne might be alive," Meagan argued, her words full of self-recrimination. "I never acted that way before. I was always the first to take up a challenge." She had related to Penny all that happened, risking rejection in her need to seek guidance from this woman she'd come to admire so greatly.

"Any woman who'd suffered under the hands of those despicable snakes would have been just as frightened and fled. And hidden, if they were able. When people live through terrifying experiences, some react in ways from which they cannot refrain and never expected, contrary to their nature. I did. Some weeks ago, I encountered two such scoundrels, the likes of what happened to you. Had Derek not arrived in time and scared them off, I might have suffered the same fate as your mother. The girls and I both."

Meagan eyed Penny in shock, wondering if she referred to one of the miners Meagan had glimpsed once she left her room. Most men at the hotel steered clear of her, though they did a lot of curious staring, likely because they thought her demented. A few had been kind, while still others leered at her much as those men at the river had done. She shivered, grateful for Clay, who she'd learned had slept outside her cubicle as her guard.

"Was this at the hotel?" she asked Penny.

"No. Before Silverton. I thought I might travel farther west to Carson City. Derek acted as our guide. One morning, the girls and I were at the campsite. I made breakfast while Derek visited a hot spring." Her voice was hollow as she recalled that time, and a furrow formed between her brows. "Two horsemen rode up to me and the girls, taunting us. One tried to have his way with me, and Derek shot at them from where he'd kept hidden." A wistful smile tilted her mouth. "My husband is clever with a gun and warned the two away quite successfully."

"I just wish I'd warned Ma." Meagan's gaze fell to her lap. It helped to know that she'd not accidentally started the fire. Nonetheless, her burden of guilt weighed almost as heavy as before.

"Meagan, you cannot be blamin' yourself. 'Tis a crying shame what happened, and we're all aggrieved for your loss, but you cannot be shoulderin' the blame."

"I disobeyed her."

Penny shook her head in confusion. "What?"

"Ma told me to fetch water and be quick about it." Meagan bowed her head. "But I got caught up in daydreams. It wasn't the first time. And this"—she lifted her bandaged hands from her lap—"is my punishment."

"Punishment?" Penny's tone was incredulous. "From whom?"

Meagan blinked her way. "The Almighty God, of course. Clay read to me how He punished the children of disobedience. He allowed them to be stolen from their homes, and all manner of destruction came against them."

"Clay read that to you, did he?" Penny again shook her head, slowly this time, her expression amazed and exasperated. "I suppose I should have urged him to start with the New

Testament—an accounting of Jesus and the covenant God gave through Him, His Son. A new covenant." She laid her hand on Meagan's forearm. "God is not desiring to destroy you, Meagan. On the contrary—He wants to save you from destruction. He wants you to know Him."

Meagan felt confused. "But I disobeyed Ma. That's why she and Wayne are dead. If I'd only done as I ought, they could have at least been prepared to fight off those men."

"What else could you have done? Run the other way and let those hooligans chase you home? It might have gone worse if you had—you might also be in the grave." Her eyes shone intently. "Mind you, I don't condone disobedience. At times, lately, it's been a trial getting my own girls to behave—and not only at fetching water. 'Tis a fault many children tend to share." Her tone came light, wry, and Meagan sensed she tried to ease her remorse. "Truth be told, if God decided to punish or do away with the children who defied their parents at one time or another, I strongly doubt the earth would be inhabited." She chuckled. "But I love my girls dearly and would never cause them harm. As much as I love them, God loves His children with a love far greater. Enough to sacrifice His life to save a sinful mankind—those who would repent of their evil ways and follow Him and His teachings."

"But it said in that book that the people who disobeyed were punished," Meagan insisted.

"Aye, but if you take notice, those were the ones who chose to worship foreign images and idols rather than their true Creator. Their sin was great because they turned from God to worship His creations instead of Himself and His teachings. And we both know what happens to those here in the West who defy the law."

Meagan nodded, a ray of understanding beginning to dawn in her mind.

"God did warn His children of the dire consequences, many times. But their hearts were hard, and they turned away. That's why they suffered. Their disobedience was continual and without remorse. Yet even then, God loved them so that each time they repented He answered their cries and delivered them from their persecutions."

Meagan brooded over Penny's words. She'd known that God existed but always thought of Him as somewhere high in the clouds, distant, with too much to do above to pay much attention to the people below. Yet the words Clay had read and Penny now uttered described a God who involved Himself in His children's lives and cared about their choices.

It was an unsettling thought.

"Do you remember when you first came to us, I told you the good Lord can—and will—forgive you of any wrongdoing?" Penny broke the silence that had arisen.

Meagan gave a distracted nod.

"Well, then." She squeezed her arm again. "All you have to do is ask Him." Penny slid to the ground and wrapped her half-eaten sandwich in its brown paper. "I advise taking up your next reading in the Gospel of Matthew."

"I don't know how to read."

Penny looked at her. "Is that a fact? Often I forget how blessed I am that my da knew and taught me." She smiled. "If you're wantin', I can teach you."

As wide as she opened her eyes, Meagan felt them burn. "You'd do that? Despite all I've done?"

"All you've done?" Penny looked confused again.

Meagan glanced down. "I was sure you'd come to despise me once you knew the truth. And Cl—the others, too." She just prevented herself from blurting out Clay's name, but with the manner in which Penny's eyes lit up, Meagan guessed she hadn't been fooled. "It was one of the reasons I was afraid to recall all that happened. I didn't want you throwing me out. When we were at the hotel."

"Throwing you out? Goodness, no! And the 'others' have no cause to look spitefully at you, not that they would. The good Lord said to a mob ready to stone a woman that he who was without sin should cast the first stone. Needless to say, those men dropped their stones without further ado." Penny's smile was infectious, making Meagan grin. "I cannot think of a soul in our party able to wield a rock had they been there. One young man in particular. Stubbornness can be as much a sin as disobedience, and he has it without measure." Penny frowned.

Meagan doubted she spoke of her husband or Kurt. Twice she'd glimpsed Penny speak with Clay; neither time had Penny looked happy when she left his company. Meagan wondered what sin of stubbornness Clay must have committed.

Penny's brow smoothed again. "If you're of a mind to do so, I could read to you and teach you letters. I brought the Holy Book with me. Never would I think of leaving it behind."

"I'd appreciate that. But I wouldn't want to keep you from the others."

"I offered," she reminded with a gentle smile. "Besides. . ." She climbed back in the wagon with a little grunt. "That is one meeting I've no wish to attend!"

At her curious words bordering on grim exasperation, Meagan lifted her brows but didn't ask Penny to explain.

❧

Clay stood, hands on his hips, and stared at the crackling fire. Derek, Kurt, and Linda sat around its warmth, discussing the mine, as they'd been doing for a good fifteen minutes. Nearby, Livvie pitched stones in the river with her slingshot while Christa watched. Penny and Meagan sat inside the wagon where they'd been for the past hour, doing who knew what, and Clay didn't wish to interfere. Though his sister-in-law could be a trial, she could also be a blessing, and Meagan needed comfort. Comfort Clay wished he had the right to give.

He kicked at a clump of undergrowth. He couldn't very well go for a walk to remove himself from the small gathering—the sun would make its full disappearance soon and it would be too dark to see. His little nieces seemed withdrawn when he'd tried to get them to speak—likely tired from the day's travel. And so he was stuck with the others by the fire and privy to their conversation.

"Claim jumpers?" Derek asked in response to information Kurt just revealed. "I hadn't thought of that. The clerk in Silverton didn't give me reason to believe we had anything to worry about—didn't say much at all, as a matter of fact."

"I just thought I'd bring it up after what Meagan said earlier. That's why her stepfather left their family behind. To protect his claim from such vagrants, much good that it did."

A melancholy lull passed, and Derek wondered if claim jumpers had killed Meagan's kin. Still, it didn't make much sense that they would burn down the house and leave the area if they'd stolen the claim.

"I'll check with the clerk once we get back to Silverton," Derek said. "Or maybe I won't have to. . . . We could continue west in search of the mine, bein' as how we're this far along. Plenty of game to keep us well fed, and Penny brought along extra blankets. I have my bedroll, and Clay has his."

"I'm fine with the arrangement," Kurt agreed. "I have Linda's part of the map on my person. Never go anywhere without it."

"And I have mine. Not sure about Clay though."

Clay didn't want to join their conversation; neither did he like being a third party and discussed as if he weren't there. He spoke up.

"Sorry, plans won't work. I need to return to Silverton and

attempt getting a message to Meagan's stepfather in Carson City. She has no one else in this world, and the man has to be told what happened someday soon."

"But I thought...," Linda began as if confused.

"What? What did you think?" Clay struggled to keep his frustration in check.

"Nothing." She looked into the fire.

Kurt frowned but didn't say a word, except to whisper something near Linda's ear. She nodded, and the two rose. "Whatever you decide is fine with us," Kurt said to Derek and nodded to him in parting, ignoring Clay. The couple left, Kurt's arm around Linda's waist, their heads together as they talked.

Clay supposed he could follow them to the wagon, despite Kurt's irritation, and see what Meagan and Penny were up to...though he still burned from his earlier conversation with his opinionated sister-in-law and had no real desire to speak with her. Best to just turn in early.

Ignoring Derek, he retrieved his bedroll from his horse and threw the parcel to the ground near the fire. Derek hadn't moved from his spot. At least he remained quiet, and Clay felt thankful for small favors.

Clay worked the knots loose from the twine and spread out the thick canvas but felt too alert to sleep. He needed something to occupy his mind, to get his thoughts off Meagan and her troubles and away from the silent dark figure staring at him from across the fire. With nothing more to do and wanting to seem occupied, he fished out his map portion from his jacket, unfolded it, and stared out over the river to the hills farther west. Perusing the snaky line he assumed was supposed to symbolize the river, he followed it to the point of the *X*. Too bad there wasn't much else to go on for his third of the map.

"No use searching in these parts," Derek said, breaking over the peaceful sound of the crackling fire. "You have to pass Three Leaning Rocks, and we've yet to reach it. Penny and I found the place on our journey. It's about another eight days' west."

His mouth tight, Clay folded his map. Not that he believed Derek farther than he could throw him, but all interest waned at his brother's interference.

Derek released a weary breath. "Given any thought as to what you might do once we find the mine?"

Clay shrugged.

"I'd like to offer a suggestion." Derek's words came slow, hesitant, as if testing the waters of Clay's cooperation to listen. When Clay didn't respond, Derek went on. "As you know, Penny and I plan on starting a ranch. Raise some cattle. Our homestead is in a pretty little valley, with a stream running near the shanty. Once we locate the silver, I plan to build a bigger place, hire some hands to help run it. If you haven't made plans for the future, you might consider taking up with us."

Derek wanted him to be a ranch hand? To *work* for him and *serve* him? Of all the low, twisted, and cruel. . .

Watching his face, Derek quickly added, "I want us to be partners, Clay. Even thought of a name for the place, if you're agreeable—the B & B Ranch, for Burke Brothers. I'd like us to live and work side by side, carve out a good life for our families." Derek smiled, clearly taken with the notion. "I reckon you plan on starting one soon, what with the way I've seen you look at Meagan. I know you spend a good amount of time in her company."

Clay felt the heat brand his face. Were his feelings so transparent that everyone thought the two of them should be hitched, from the youngest Burke to the oldest?

"I regret the years we lost, and I want to make a fresh start. You're the only brother I have, and I don't want to lose you, like we lost our ma. And Pa, too."

It was the wrong thing to say. Like a flame to dry tinder, all the bad memories blazed to life and burned inside Clay's mind. "I haven't taken handouts from you since the day I was old enough to manage on my own, not a single one, and I don't intend starting now, *brother*." He said the last in a cutting way.

Derek flinched as though struck. "At least take some time to think about it."

"I've had *four years*." Clay stressed the last two words, making his message clear. "I've done all the thinking necessary."

"Then I reckon there's nothing more to say." Derek's voice came low.

"You're right about that."

Clay noticed his brother moved slower than usual as he gave a slight nod and rose to his feet like an old man whose bones had withered with age. Any smattering of triumph evaded him, and Clay felt hateful, petty. The time spent in his brother's company these past weeks hadn't eliminated his animosity, but it had been enough to shave off the rough edges and wasn't wholly intolerable.

Clay thought back. With his own eyes, he observed some of the changes Derek had admitted to. His tender affections toward Penny, his devotion toward their girls, his ability to sit and listen to an old, homesick miner pour out his problems— whereas the old Derek in his restlessness wouldn't have noticed the old man, much less offered helpful advice. Clay despised the envy that tightened his chest when he witnessed the consideration Derek so often gave others, where before he'd had little of the same kindness to grant his own kin. Clay's state of mind had led him to speak sharper than he might have done if he hadn't been so annoyed, to the point he almost was willing to call his brother back and apologize.

Almost.

He had little time to dwell on his own shortcomings as,

without warning, a shower of ice-cold water streamed over his head in a blinding torrent.

"What the. . . !" Blinking hard and wiping the stinging water from his eyes, he noted Christa and Livvie had turned from the river and stared up behind him, their mouths hanging wide open, and he managed to stifle the rest of his oath. He jumped to his feet, swinging around to face the culprit.

Penny's eyes blazed as she held the rim of the empty water bucket in one hand. "Linda may fear a rift between the two of you should she speak, what with your differences so newly mended, and my dear husband may continue playin' the martyr, feeling he's deservin' of your ill will—but I've had enough of your balderdash, Clayton Burke. I have a great deal to say, and you'll stand there and listen to every word!"

Clay gaped at his normally sane sister-in-law, still too befuddled to form a retort. His mind felt numb and senseless, frozen by the chill—from both her dour expression and the river water.

"Show me a man who never makes mistakes, and I'll show you a man stone cold in his grave," Penny sputtered, her brogue strong. "Your pigheadedness is causing this family a good deal of strife and heartache, and 'tis high time you put a stop to it. Your brother has done his utmost to make amends, but I do believe you get a perverse joy out of seeing him suffer." She threw down the bucket with a sideways thrust, keeping her snapping eyes fixed on him. "There'll be an end to that, as well. I love you as if you were blood kin, but no longer will I tolerate such nonsense. If you're wantin' to be sharin' with others your harsh behavior, you may as well make your home in these parts, among other creatures of the wild—but if it's human companionship you're after, then I advise you to start behaving like one!"

With a whirl of her skirts, she swept off toward the wagon.

Kurt stood nearby, as transfixed as Clay. Derek approached from some distance, his expression stunned as he took in Clay's appearance. Clearly he struggled over what to say or do. "I, uh, apologize. She's in the family way, and her moods have taken on a mind of their own. One minute she's singing like a mockingbird; the next, spitting like a wildcat. I best go check on her." With an uneasy nod, he strode to where his wife had disappeared.

The girls gaped at Clay, then took off running after their parents. Kurt shook his head and also turned to the wagon, just as Linda came hurrying from the back.

"Here." She thrust one of the blankets at Clay. "It's not much, but it'll help you dry off before the cold sets in."

If that was all she was worried about, she was too late. He had already started to shiver as twilight chilled the air that the sun's warmth had abandoned. "Thanks." He took the blanket.

She seemed nervous as she watched him towel off with half of the long length of wool. He was thankful to note his bedroll had received almost none of the downpour.

"I've never seen her act so upset," Linda said after a moment.

Clay thought the matter over and sighed. "She had good reason, I suppose."

"You two don't get along?"

"We have our moments." Clay tossed the damp blanket by the fire. "Usually when she brings up one of two subjects: God or the silver mine, and what I need to do about both."

Linda studied him, then looked toward the river.

Recalling Penny's accusations, he sighed. "You have something you want to say? You needn't be afraid to come out and say whatever's on your mind, Linda. It sure can't be any worse than Penny's methods." He kept his tone light and inviting. The last thing he wanted was for any woman to fear him, especially his own kin.

"It's just that. . ." She hesitated. "It's odd how we didn't meet till recently, but both of us suffered the same misfortune: We both had only our mothers to rely on as children, and our mothers were taken away too soon by disease. But each of us reacted so differently to the loss. Losing my mother made me yearn to draw close to what she believed in and find God, while you did the exact opposite when your ma died and refused to have anything to do with Him."

"I don't know if I'd go that far. . . ." Her words rang dead true, making him ill at ease. Memory of the recent scripture he'd read to Meagan only aggravated the problem. God punished those Old Testament people who'd turned from Him and His precepts and in a manner that made Clay cringe inside. Bondage, starvation, even death. . .

"Well, I don't know what else you'd call it," she insisted, her tone and eyes anxious, not argumentative.

"Don't worry about me, Linda." He smiled with forced confidence and bluster. "I've taken care of myself a good many years, and I'll go on doing just fine."

"Will you?" she insisted. "I'm not so sure. It's just that. . ." She drew her shawl closer around her shoulders. "We're family. Now that we've found each other, there's no reason for you to live life alone. I want you to be happy, too, Clay, and I sense you're far from it. I want to share with you what I've found. . . ." Her brow wrinkled.

His heart softened at her hesitant words. "That means more to me than I can say."

"Does it?" She looked unconvinced. She moved toward the river and stared into the dark water. "May I speak frankly?" she asked, turning to face him.

He tensed but nodded.

"You can't see them well now, but ever notice how the rocks beneath the water are smooth, their sharp edges worn down?

But the rocks outside the current. . ." She looked to the rocks scattered near her feet. Picking one up, she held it out. "They're hard and stony, sharp. Some dry as dust and easily crumbled."

"Guess that's why they call them rocks," Clay joked, and she smiled.

"Did you know in the Good Book the Lord said He's like streams of living water and in Him, you'll never thirst? If I had my choice, I'd rather be immersed in His living water, letting His love shape me and soften the coarse edges, than just lying within reach, but on the outside—the heat and sun baking me hard and dry." She looked at him, awaiting his response.

"If I had my choice, I'd rather not be a rock—though Pa often said my head was full of them." His little joke came out feeble, her words affecting him more than he let on.

Her lips smiled, but her eyes remained sad. "Well, that's all I wanted to share. It's something that came to me as we were sitting here earlier and I was looking at the river. I should go help Penny."

"Linda," he said before she could leave.

She regarded him in question.

"Thanks for sharing that with me. Having a sister is as nice as I hoped it might be."

Her eyes lit up at his compliment, and she smiled and nodded before moving away. Clay watched her go, then turned to gaze into the river and what little he could see of the stones beneath.

Deep in thought, he didn't move until he heard a step directly behind him. He quickly turned, leery after Penny's recent dousing.

Meagan came to a swift halt, her eyes as clouded as the earlier sky.

nine

Clay regarded Meagan, his manner cautious. She felt bad about startling him. "Sorry, I should've spoken—"

"No harm done," he reassured. "Feeling better?"

"All things considering. I just wanted to warm myself by the fire. . . ." Meagan's words trailed off as she noticed his wet shirt and dripping hair. Surely he had hadn't taken a swim in the river with his clothes on, and with the cold night approaching! Had he fallen in?

With a wry grin, he grabbed a hank of his hair and squeezed water from the long strands. "A gift from my sister-in-law. Guess she thought I needed cooling down."

"Penny did that to you?" Meagan could scarcely believe the gentle friend who'd been so gracious to her only minutes before could do such a shocking thing. Upon leaving the wagon, Penny had grabbed the pail off a hook, expressing the need for water. Meagan had been so absorbed with her exciting new undertaking of learning to read she hadn't paid attention to the group at the river.

"Something I said." Clay shrugged. "Or didn't say. One can never tell with her."

Meagan searched for a suitable reply. "I hope you work out your differences."

"I doubt that'll happen." At her curious stare, he released a weary breath. "She's angry because I won't see things her way with regard to my brother." He looked toward the river, clearly uncomfortable.

"It's all right," she reassured him. "You can talk about your brother in my company. I'm not made of glass. I won't break."

His eyes gentled as he turned her way. "No, you're not, are you? Fact is, you're one of the strongest women I've run across. You exhibited courage going back there today. Even to pay last respects, I'm not sure many women would have done the same if they thought there could be danger."

"You think there still is?"

"No. Our fears were groundless. But I can't help but wonder what you'll do once those bandages come off your hands."

He seemed uneasy, and she put into words what he didn't say. "You mean if I'm crippled, if I don't regain good use of my hands."

"Penny thinks you will, and she's a better authority than I am with all her cures," he was quick to offer.

Meagan nodded, lifting her hands to look at them. "Yet I would gladly give both if I could have my family back. Even Wayne, trial that he was. It seems we fought every day, but I still miss him." She looked at Clay. "I suppose I didn't appreciate what I had till it was taken from me. Now it's gone and I have nothing left."

Clay winced. "What about your stepfather?"

"I don't imagine he'll care much one way or the other. He'll mind that his shack is gone and the things he'd left behind. But he didn't care much for me or Wayne, and I doubt he had fond feelings for Ma."

"I'm sorry."

"Don't be." Meagan attempted a careless shrug. "I'm just grateful I had my parents' love. Some people don't. Pa—my true pa—was often ill, but he made me feel special."

"You are."

"What?" Meagan looked at him in surprise.

"Special." His face flushed a shade darker.

Tongue-tied, she could only stare.

Clay moved a few steps toward the river. "What will you do now?"

With so much to endure, Meagan hadn't given the future much thought. "I don't know. I never learned a trade befitting a woman—never was good at sewing, but I don't suppose Silverton has much use for a seamstress, even if I am able to hold a needle again. The little I saw, your town was teeming with men and very few women."

"It's not my town."

"Pardon?"

"I'm only traveling through. I don't plan on staying."

"Oh." That he would one day leave had never occurred to Meagan. She wondered why he would want to go and when, felt upset that he planned to, but masked her feelings. "Penny is teaching me my letters and how to read. I'm not sure what good that'll do me—it's nice to learn, but really, I don't know what I'll do."

For the first time, Meagan realized she wasn't much use at all. Clay was wrong; she wasn't special. In a mining town, she didn't know how she would manage, especially without Clay to go to for advice or company. She had come to expect his presence, his friendship. However would she even survive in such a place? She could never give herself to men like the saloon and dance-hall prostitutes did. She pondered the idea of traveling farther west to a big city like Carson City. She imagined that, no matter the size of the locale, she would face similar problems.

"Do you have family back East?"

"No. It's just me."

The sudden knowledge of what that meant terrified her, though she tried to remain strong. Clay must have heard the catch in her voice; he turned to look, then walked her way again. Whatever unease had sprung up between them dissolved as she moved into his open arms. His shirt was cold and damp, causing her to shiver, but his hands were warm at her back, his embrace comforting as she melted against him. Held close against his strength, her fears began to ebb.

"Meagan, it'll be all right," he soothed. "We're not going to leave you floundering, I promise. Never would I do that to you. You're not alone in this world, no matter how you feel at the moment." His strong arms tightened around her as if afraid she might try to move away.

She had no intention of moving a muscle. His fingers spread slightly and stroked her hair, and the memory of being carried in his arms drifted to her. She smiled against his shirt, never feeling so safe as when she was near him, so close she could feel his breaths and the beating of his heart. But unlike the first time, she suffered no fatigue, and her senses remained alert. Her heart stirred, and she held her breath, hoping by doing so she could force time to still. That he might hold her like this forever. . .

He retreated a fraction, and she wanted to protest; his eyes met hers, and she forgot all else. She immersed herself in their deep blue, darker now with night approaching. Lost in their depths, she did not want to struggle to save herself from drowning, wishing only to sink further as the seconds froze into eternity.

His gaze lowered to her mouth the moment before his cool lips brushed hers, his kiss so gentle it might have been no more than the touch of a feather, the effect so forceful she felt as if a feather could knock her to her knees. She closed her eyes and gripped his damp sleeves. Sweet warmth coursed through her in rivulets, the chill of his wet clothing forgotten. His arms tightened around her. His mouth, now warm, pressed more firmly against hers, making her heart pound so loud she heard it in her ears, when suddenly he moved away.

Where seconds before his gaze had been intent, now he seemed incapable of looking at her except for the briefest of glances.

Meagan sensed his nervous state was the forerunner to an apology. Though she also felt awkward, she couldn't bear for him to sum up a long-anticipated moment into a thoughtless mistake. Her first kiss, her only kiss, but if it must be their last, she would not have it sullied by hurtful memories of his remorse.

"Meagan, I. . ."

"The night has a chill, more so than I thought," she interrupted, "and the fire isn't as warm as it looks. I should retire and leave you to your drying out." Foolish words, but Meagan barely knew what she said, only that she must speak so he would not.

She turned to go, but his hand on her arm stopped her. A little shiver went through her when she recalled how only moments before that same hand had pressed against her spine and his gentle fingers had woven through her hair.

"Meagan, please don't go away angry."

"I'm not." She shouldn't look at him but couldn't help herself. The pain and regret swimming in his eyes lanced an arrow through her heart. She must go before he completely ruined whatever happiness remained.

"Honest, I'm all right. Please, Clay. Let me go."

"I never meant to hurt you. That's the last thing I wanted to do."

Then don't say another word. She attempted a smile to mask the cry that begged to peal from her throat. "I'm just tired. It's been a long day, and tomorrow will be another."

"Of course." He released her arm. "I apologize. I didn't mean to keep you."

"You didn't. Good night."

Meagan hurriedly walked away. She wanted to race to the dark solitude offered in the wagon bed but feared doing so would alert the others that something was wrong. And something was definitely wrong.

She should have known better than to kiss him, to let his kiss linger, should have pushed him aside. But her foolish heart had yearned for this for days.

If only she could turn back the sun, erase those last moments. But time flew ever onward, and she wondered what difficult cost of suffering the future days might exact from her for her mistake in thinking Clay returned her love.

※

In the darkness settling around their camp, Clay could barely see the rocks Linda had pointed out earlier. Maybe Pa had been right, and his head was full of them.

Had he frightened Meagan, upset her, or both? He'd had no right to kiss her, and she'd made it pretty clear she wished he hadn't. He'd never planned or intended to follow through with what had been revolving inside his head since she joined him. He'd thought her soft lips had answered his gentle quest and she wanted him to continue, but he must have imagined it. What an unfeeling rogue she must think him! After all she'd suffered—then to crown her nightmarish day by shocking her with his unwelcome affections. . . .

Sighing, he picked up the blanket, using the drier half to rub at his damp clothes. The fire wasn't doing the trick, not working as fast as he would like. And he didn't relish the idea of sleeping in this condition.

Footsteps crunched through the scrub, and he darted a wary glance over his shoulder.

"Looks like you got a heap of women troubles," Kurt said in greeting.

Clay eyed him with reservation, wondering if he addressed

Clay as friend or foe. The deputy made no mystery that he sided with Derek in the quarrel between brothers.

Kurt lifted his hands in the air. "I come in peace. Between Penny's dousing and what I just saw, you looked like you could use a friend."

"What you saw. . ." Clay left the words hanging, fishing for exactly what Kurt had seen.

The deputy put his hands down. "You kissing Meagan. The both of you sharing words. Her rushing off upset."

Clay's face blazed as he continued toweling dry with the blanket. He'd thought the others too immersed in their own nighttime tasks to take any notice of him or Meagan. He should have known better.

"I saw Linda giving you a peace of her mind earlier, too," Kurt continued when Clay didn't respond.

"At least she was kind about it."

"Really?"

Clay looked at his brother-in-law. "I imagine my sister is one of the meekest and most gentle women I've met."

Kurt snorted. "Meek? Linda?"

"That's the impression I got."

"That's because she's trying so hard to be cautious around you. Give it time." Kurt chuckled. "Don't misunderstand. I love my wife, but she can be as much of a wildcat as Penny. Fact is, the day I met Linda, she pulled a derringer on me. When I wrestled it from her, she clawed and kicked to escape—even knocked me in the jaw." He grinned and settled his hands on his hips. "Of course, she had just discovered I was the law and only doing my duty. She didn't take too kindly to me at first, especially when I took her as my prisoner and locked her up in the jailhouse. At the time, I thought she was a young hellion with a weakness for breaking the law."

Clay raised his brows in amazement. Linda had neglected

to fill him in on a good deal of what happened after she disappeared from Silverton.

The deputy shook his head. "Just goes to show we can't always judge by first encounters. She was none of those things. Well, except spirited—she still is that—and at times impossible. She definitely has a will of her own."

"Yeah, she does," Clay agreed. "It's that stubborn Burke blood."

Kurt chuckled. "I imagine I was wrong about you, too. In watching you with Meagan since you brought her to Silverton, I've noticed something good and noble about you that I hadn't thought existed."

"Not after talking to Derek, you mean?" Clay asked wryly.

"I form my own judgments. I don't need others telling me how I should feel."

Clay gave a short nod. "Good to know."

"The first night we met," Kurt drawled, "I saw two sides of the same man. The side who would sacrifice everything for a woman in need, and the side who would sacrifice his brother to meet his own needs."

Clay snorted. "Not that ornery, I trust. I may have been fuming, but I wouldn't wish Derek dead."

"Glad to hear it. I'm not always sure when I hear you talk. Thing is—"

Clay's gaze flicked beyond Kurt a moment, the rustle of skirts warning of someone's approach. Kurt's attention returned to Clay. "A man can't satisfy both sides and be at peace. Either he's got a good heart, or he doesn't, and a man with a good heart can't live in any sort of true peace and despise his brother. There's a time to put an end to bitterness, Clay. For your sake. And to ask yourself which man you want to be."

Resigned to his entire family trying to interfere in his quarrel with Derek, Clay gave a tired nod. Each day that passed, his defenses wore down a little more. "I'll keep that in mind."

"Do that. The man I saw taking such devoted care of a lady in distress these past weeks is a man I'd like to call friend."

Penny came into view, and Kurt nodded a farewell to both Clay and his sister-in-law. "Evenin'." He walked away, and Penny advanced.

Before Kurt was out of earshot, Penny began, her eyes snapping. "I had full well intended to come to you with an apology—"

"I accept."

"That is, till I put the children to bed and saw that poor girl in tears, hiding in the wagon."

"Meagan?" His heart plummeted to hear she'd been that upset.

"Who else? I tried talking with her, but she won't speak of what ails her. What did you say to make her cry?"

His tattered defenses rose to the fore. "Must you always assume the worst when it comes to me?"

"You were the last one with her. I've heard the sting of your words to your own brother this night, so don't give me that righteous attitude, Clayton Burke. Bitterness has a way of spreading to those not deserving of it. And you were as bitter as a dill pickle."

Her comparison amused him, puncturing a hole in his temper. "I didn't say anything to hurt her." He wanted to suggest that Meagan might still be upset over the days' events and mourning her family or better yet, not say a word, but his tongue played traitor and admitted the truth before he could think twice. "I kissed her, if you must know." Again his face burned flame hot.

Penny gaped at him in disbelief. "Kissed her?" she repeated below her breath. "And you no more than an hour ago telling us you doona intend on courting her? You would trifle with such a sweet girl's affections like that?"

He wondered if he should just jump in the river and save Penny the trouble of fetching the bucket.

"First," he said ruefully, "I would never do a thing to harm her. Second, I never intended it to happen."

"And that's supposed to excuse such behavior, is it?"

He grimaced and crossed his arms over his chest. "I tried apologizing, but she wouldn't let me."

"Perhaps you didn't try hard enough."

Letting out a sigh, Clay closed his eyes. Maybe he hadn't. Fact was, he wasn't one bit sorry he'd kissed Meagan—only that she'd been offended. And yes, he'd told the others that he didn't intend on courting her, but in that moment, even before the kiss, he'd questioned such a decision.

"I know you care for Meagan and would never willfully hurt her—anyone with two eyes can see that." Penny's tone gentled. "But if you've made up your mind there's no future for the two of you to share, then you must do what is in her best interests. Especially now. She's so fragile after all that's happened."

"What do you recommend?"

Penny shook her head in dismay. "As much as I hate to say it, you shouldn't keep company with her any longer, not as you've done. When a man kisses a woman, a decent woman, 'tis a sign he wants to extend their friendship. To spend time with her after tonight will only confuse and injure her further when you do pull away."

Clay didn't want to admit it, but she made sense. Nor did he want to think of the day when he must leave Meagan, but Penny was right about that, too. He had no desire to put down roots in Silverton; once he knew Meagan would be safe and prosper in her new life, he had every intention of searching for the mine.

Yet thoughts of leaving her rankled him. He didn't see how she could survive with her scarred hands that may never regain full use, with no family to care for her, in a mining town of gruff men, the only womenfolk for company being ladies of the evening. He winced, then thought of Beulah. Despite her chosen profession, she had a gentle heart. Perhaps he should introduce her to Meagan, then wondered how. He didn't intend to step foot inside a saloon or dance hall again, and Beulah rarely left the one where she worked. On second thought, Beulah might influence Meagan unfavorably, and he couldn't stand the thought of her resorting to an immoral life. Silverton was no place for Meagan, either.

Clearly expecting a reply, Penny continued staring. "And you don't think it will hurt her to put distance between us?" he asked.

"It will hurt her a good deal more if you don't."

Something occurred to Clay. "That is, assuming she has feelings for me. Like as not, she doesn't, in which case this conversation is moot, though I do owe her an apology."

She studied him as if he spoke a foreign language. "You're smarter than that, Clay. You're not ignorant even if you do have a few ignorant ideas. Surely you're not blind to the fact that she lights up like a sunbeam whenever you walk into a room."

"I assumed she was happy to see a new face."

"She never responded in such a manner whenever Linda or I entered."

Penny's words both delighted and distressed him. To learn Meagan might conceal the same depth of affection for Clay gave him hope they could share a future together, but the truth of his bleak situation immediately scattered it. He had nothing to offer her: no home, no money, no material goods. Once he found the mine, those circumstances could change, but Derek had questioned the silver's existence more than once. Much as Clay hated to admit it, his brother could be right. Their pa had been a liar and at times played cruel jokes. Maybe this was all an elaborate prank, and they only wasted their time.

He expelled his frustration somewhere between a sigh and a groan. "Agreed. I'll stay away."

"It wouldn't be a problem if you felt differently, but as you don't. . ." She shrugged, her manner sympathetic. "And before I'll be forgetting, I'll be giving you that apology now. I never should have let my temper get the better of me."

Clay attempted a smile. "I probably deserved it."

"Aye, but at least I might have waited for the sun to warm the sky again." Her eyes twinkled in mischief, and she squeezed him in a half hug. "Linda is putting some coffee on. That will help warm you."

He nodded, his mind already elsewhere. . .somewhere he didn't want to go. Penny left him and walked back to the wagon. Clay looked past the fire, catching sight of Derek on the other side.

ten

The reprieve Meagan hoped for got cut short as Livvie and Christa climbed into the back of the wagon, chattering as if they were again the best of friends. Meagan swiped at her wet cheeks, and the girls quieted. They looked at one another, then at Meagan. She worked to get her mouth to smile, then started as a coyote howled.

"You ain't afraid of them coyotes, are you Miss Meagan?" Livvie's question preceded another distant howl, " 'Cause there ain't no reason to fear. Uncle Kurt and Pa are good shots; don't know about Uncle Clay. And I can hit anything dead on from more'n a distance of five wagons end to end," she boasted, patting her slingshot that she'd tucked in some twine knotted around her waist.

"Livvie helped get me away from a pack of coyotes," Christa said, her big eyes shining in all seriousness. "When we was on the trail."

"Sure did," Livvie boasted. "Hit one smack on the nose. It went yipping off, and we never saw hide nor hair of it again."

"Really," Meagan said, trying to sound as if she hadn't been crying. "It sounds like you're quite handy with that slingshot, Livvie."

"And I been practicin' every day to get better. One day I'm gonna be as good as David. He was a shepherd boy before he became king, and he killed him a lion and then a giant all the men feared. But I ain't afraid of anything—just like David."

"A giant?" Meagan inquired.

"A man so tall, I reckon he's as tall as the hills."

"It's in the Holy Book Mama reads to us," Christa whispered in reverence.

"Oh." Meagan glanced at the book, where Penny had left it in the corner of the wagon. Both Penny and Clay had told her what the Bible contained weren't made-up tales but accounts of actual occurrences. Penny had read to her from the New Testament earlier, which told of the Lord Jesus in such an appealing manner that Meagan was no longer certain of God's punishment toward her; instead she wanted to know more about the Son of Man—also the Son of God—whose humble beginnings in a stable brought kings to kneel before Him. He walked among the people, teaching them day and night, never too weary to heal their bodies, always giving of Himself and His love. She could use a good dose of all three of His gifts. She imagined He wouldn't fear a giant either, though she'd never want to run up against a man so tall!

"I'm not afraid, Livvie. Not of coyotes at any rate."

"If you're not afraid, what are you?"

"Pardon?"

"Why are you hiding in here and not outside with Mama and Linda?"

"And Uncle Clay," Christa added. "Don't you like him no more?"

"Sure I do. I mean. . ." Her face grew warm. "I suppose I'm just sad after all that's happened. And going back to where I once lived made it worse."

Christa pulled her doll from a nearby blanket where it had been tucked in up to its cloth neck. "Would you like to hold Ruby again?"

Meagan stared at the curious, shining faces of the two little girls she'd come to care for as family. "You know what I'd really like?"

Christa shook her head.

"A big hug." She tentatively held her arms out to the girls in invitation.

They rushed toward her and wrapped their arms around her. The momentum sent them ~~flying backward, and Meagan's~~ head and shoulders hit the canvas cover. As she slid down, she heard the wooden rib nearest her creak in protest and hoped it wouldn't splinter. The girls' giggles were infectious, and Meagan joined in as she lay there with them sprawled on top of her.

"Well, and just what mischief have I come upon?" Penny's cheery voice broke through the giggling. "What are the two of you doing to poor Miss Meagan?"

The girls let go and sat up. "We weren't doing nothin' wrong, Mama," Livvie hurried to say. "Honest!"

"I'm to blame," Meagan explained, not wanting the girls in trouble.

"Never you mind. It's good to see you smile." She looked from Meagan to her girls. "Now then, go tell your pa good night."

"Are we in trouble?" Christa asked.

"You will be if you don't mind." Penny gave her youngest a gentle tap on the nose. "Your pa said he might play the harmonica, but only if you hurry and do as you're told."

With excited squeals, the children scrambled from the wagon.

"I brought coffee." Penny offered Meagan a tin cup she held. "I thought it would help take the chill off."

"Thank you." Grateful, Meagan scooted to the rear of the wagon, took the steaming cup, and sipped the strong, black brew. A wash of heat rushed through her veins, and she sighed in contentment.

"Have you given any thought to your future?" Penny climbed inside.

"Not much."

"I have something I'd like to discuss. Something I talked over with Derek. He'll be leaving soon with Linda and Kurt on a trip farther west, and we've decided I should return to the homestead with the girls. The journey might be too harsh for Christa—of late I've had reservations about taking her more than a day's journey—and well. . ." Her cheeks flushed. "I'm expecting a wee babe come midwinter—all the more reason Derek and I wish to move to our homestead soon."

Meagan smiled. "I'm happy for you both."

"God has indeed blessed us, but I had a reason for speaking so. If you've a mind to consider it, I want you to come and stay with us."

Meagan's mouth dropped open in shock as fresh tears wet her eyes at so generous an invitation. "I don't know what to say. I wouldn't want to impose."

"There now, don't cry." Penny's voice shook, and she dabbed at her own eyes. "You'll get me started. It's bad enough my emotions are all in a tizzy these days." She laughed. "Truly, it would be no imposition to have you stay. No one lives for miles around except miners, and though Derek has made his position clear to them and I don't foresee any more problems, I would feel better having another woman nearby."

"I don't know how much help I can be." Meagan ruefully stared at her bandaged hands. She could now manage a cup, though it was a trial holding a fork, and she still needed assistance at the most mundane of tasks.

"Even if you do nothing but keep me company, I would consider it a blessing. The days are getting longer and can be lonely without adult companionship. And the girls have taken a liking to you, as well."

"When you put it like that, I don't see how I can refuse."

"Wonderful!" Penny brightened. "I'll continue with teaching

you to read, perhaps even to write."

"How long do the others plan on being away?" Meagan hoped Penny wouldn't think her rude but needed an idea of how long her stay might last. She felt foolish for fretting over what she might do once she left the Burke home but couldn't keep from it.

Penny averted her gaze, seeming a mite distracted. "There's no way of telling. It could be a matter of weeks, even months."

"Then they're going in search of the mine?"

Penny looked at her sharply, and Meagan knew she'd said something wrong. "Where did you hear of that?"

"I overheard the girls talk. I'm sorry."

"They know?"

Meagan nodded. "They told me in Silverton. When I was laid up, they were talking to each other about it. I just hope your husband and family has better success than Landon did."

"They shouldn't have said a word." Penny's brow wrinkled in concern. "It's supposed to be kept secret."

"I'd never tell anyone."

Penny patted her arm, but Meagan could tell she was still upset. "It's not you I don't trust. If Christa or Olivia mentioned it in the wrong company. . ." She slid forward and dropped to the ground. "I must speak with Derek. Will you be all right?"

"Yes." Meagan lifted her coffee between her hands. "I have this to keep me warm."

"Ah, that reminds me. A word of caution. . ." Penny's brow relaxed. "Olivia is a restless one, even in sleep—she kicks. I often woke with bruises during our journey. And Christa is a snuggler—you may find you cannot breathe of a morning because she's found a spot atop you—but at least there's little chance you'll be cold."

"I won't mind," Meagan laughed. "When I was their age, I wished for sisters to share stories with at night. It'll be fun."

"Just don't keep them up long. I don't want them dragging their feet tomorrow."

"I won't," Meagan promised.

She watched Penny leave, sensing a small hole in her heart filled by this generous family, once more feeling as if she belonged, as if she were wanted. Her sole regret was that Clay had no desire to be included in the group who wanted her.

❧

Clay passed the night with the recent admonitions of his family battering his dreams as he searched for Meagan within them. When he found her inside a mine, she sadly acknowledged him without a word, then turned and walked away, disappearing into the thick inner darkness. He hurried to catch her, never able to, but soon realized she was only part of what he searched for—both aspirations as vital to him as air. He felt suffocated in the dank cave as he ran within its bowels, which echoed his hollow cries. Alone. Uncertain. Unable to find the exit into light and air as the blackness swallowed him into its big belly and he could no longer breathe. . . .

He woke with a start, the canvas covering his mouth and nose. Irritated, he wrenched at the top of his bedroll and straightened from his curled position, noticing no light yet filled the sky. Hearing a boot shuffle near the fire, he looked in that direction.

Derek squatted before the low flames. He grabbed the coffeepot handle, using one of Penny's cloth napkins, and poured himself a cup. His eyes flicked to Clay, and he lifted the pot, brow raised in question. Clay nodded and sat up, throwing aside his bedroll. He tipped his boots upside down and pounded the soles in case one of the high desert's occupants had decided to make its home there for the night. Finding both boots empty of snakes, lizards, or scorpions, he pulled them on, his mind wrapped up in the next few minutes. He could well imagine his ma smiling down from above, pleased that her two sons still shared the lifetime habit of waking before dawn, before anyone else in the household stirred—which now led him to this moment.

Alone with his brother, and no one else able to hear.

He tied up his bedroll, then shoved it aside and approached Derek. His brother handed him a tin of steaming, black coffee. Clay took it but remained standing.

"I watched our ma die, crying out your name over and over, almost to her last breath, and I hated you for not being there."

In the firelight, Clay took note of the sudden surprise and hope that sparked within Derek's eyes. Never in all the time since their mother's passing had Clay spoken to Derek in so deep a manner, letting his brother know his personal feelings about that awful period. Feelings he'd told no one else. He'd lambasted him for not being there but never told how it affected him.

"I used to cry when I was a boy, when I was sure no one could see or hear, wishing you'd come home and things could be like they once were. When Ma kept getting sicker, I blamed you. Since the money you sent for her medicine wasn't working to make her well, I blamed you for that, too. I figured you were just like pa and didn't care about your family. You were so rude when we met in Silverton, after having not seen each other for four years solid. Then you robbed me and Linda of our maps, I was sure you were the same sort of irascible heel our pa had been."

"Irascible?"

Clay slightly smiled. "Short-tempered. Irritable. Petulant."

"At least one of us got something out of Ma's books." Derek shook his head. "If I could live life over and undo what's been done—"

"I know. You would. Watching you with Penny and the girls

these last weeks and seeing you accept Linda, acting as her big brother, opened my eyes. You are a changed man. And Penny's right—every man makes his fair share of mistakes. But not every man is sorry for them."

"Penny spoke up for me?"

"Every day. As a matter of fact, she wouldn't let up." Clay studied the coffee in his tin. He had yet to take his first sip. "Then I couldn't stand it. Now I'm glad your wife is as persistent as she is."

"Meaning?" Derek's eyes were hopeful.

"Meaning I don't know what the future holds. I'm still not sure I can trust you enough to search for the mine together. Let's just take this a day at a time and see where the road leads." Clay sighed and took a sip of the strong brew. "Fact is, I'm tired of being your sworn enemy, like I promised you when I was nearly sixteen and you rode off, leaving me behind again, so as to take up your nomadic life."

Derek grunted in amusement. "That's what Penny called me—a nomadic drifter."

"Where do you think I got the name?" Clay asked with a smirk, taking a seat on the ground.

Derek grew serious again. "I didn't suppose you'd want to go with me, even if I'd asked. Didn't think you wanted me near you."

"Deep down, I wanted you to offer, but I never would have broken down and told you so even if you'd have threatened me with a hot branding iron. The Burke pride had its grip hard on me then. I still grapple with it."

"We're quite a pair, aren't we?" Derek shook his head and sipped his coffee. "A reformed rogue and a stubborn mule." He smiled to show he only teased.

Clay snorted. "Better than our pa, not as saintly as our ma, striving for someplace good in between."

"And Linda is the best of us three."

Clay nodded his agreement.

"At least we're striving to be better men."

"Yeah, we are at that."

No more words passed between them. Though they'd reached no real understanding, something significant had changed in their relationship. Penny noticed it when she awoke and raised her brows to see Clay sitting beside Derek. Kurt and Linda noticed it when they smiled at each other after Clay responded in a civil tone to something Derek said.

Something significant had altered between him and Meagan, too, but not for the better. When she emerged from the wagon, she barely glanced in Clay's direction and avoided him all morning.

As Derek hitched up the team, Linda packed the few items while Penny rounded up the girls who'd wandered, thrilled for the chance to play in wide-open spaces. Alone, Clay found an opportunity to speak with Meagan. But words evaded him when she turned her tawny gold eyes his way.

He searched his mind for a greeting. "Did you pass the night well?"

"Fair enough."

"That's good." Uneasy, he pulled the brim of his hat down though the morning sun shone behind. "It can get mighty cold of a night."

"We had plenty of blankets, and the girls kept me warm."

The unexpected thought of himself in their position with Meagan made his mouth go dry and tied up his tongue. Catching sight of Penny's admonishing look from afar, he again glanced at Meagan, who now eyed him strangely.

He nodded in farewell and moved to his horse, both grateful for his sister-in-law's watchful eye and perturbed by her nosy attitude. What was the harm of passing a few minutes alone with Meagan, speaking of routine affairs? Surely Penny didn't expect him to avoid her completely.

Without a doubt, staying away would not be a simple matter.

eleven

Meagan sat outside the hotel and watched Livvie take aim on an empty tin with her slingshot. Christa sat on the boardwalk nearby, taking no interest in the chair Penny had recently vacated.

Silverton appeared much as Meagan had expected a mining town to look; she'd taken only brief notice the day of the outing, and she studied the area now, hoping to see a particular face.

The area crawled with men from all walks of life, all with one shared hope of finding gold or silver and striking it rich. Canvas tents with wood fronts lined the dusty street, some belonging to tradesmen, with crude signs offering their wares, though a few all-wood buildings were in the process of being built. Near what resembled a factory, the ring of pickaxes and sledgehammers sang through the air as miners slammed their tools on a hill where a vein of silver had been found months before. And there were those adventurers who struck out to distant parts unknown, hopeful to claim a parcel of ore-filled land and become millionaires overnight, though few men had.

Meagan wondered what category Clay fit into. According to what she understood, he wished to search for their pa's mine alone. With his absence all morning, she wondered if he'd taken it into his head to leave without even a good-bye. But if he'd gone to search, surely the girls would know and be full of such news, and they hadn't spoken of their uncle at all.

Almost since the time he'd brought her to Silverton, she had witnessed Clay's animosity toward his brother but kept silent, feeling it wasn't her place to speak or offer unsolicited help. Lately, however, she'd noticed a change. The charged feeling when Clay and Derek were near one another, once as tense as a lit fuse leading to a charge of black powder, had all but disappeared.

Clay had made himself scarce since two nights before, when he'd kissed her, but when he hadn't shown up for breakfast, she worried that he'd actually left Silverton.

"Why do you keep looking up and down the street?" Christa wanted to know.

"Was I?" Meagan hedged, embarrassed to be caught. "I, um, noticed your Uncle Clay hasn't been around this morning." Meagan kept her voice detached, hoping Christa wouldn't notice her interest. "Did he leave town?"

"Why? Do you miss him?" The child's eyes danced with mysterious delight.

"I, uh, have something I want to discuss with him. In private."

"Oo–o–h–h." Christa's eyes grew rounder, as if she'd been presented with a coveted gift. "Things only the two of you should talk about that aren't fit for a small child like me to hear?"

What an odd question. But she presumed any news of Landon McClinton, which Clay might have learned by now, would be unsuitable for young ears, and nodded.

Christa squealed and clapped her hands, further confusing Meagan.

"He's probably talking to Miss Beulah," Livvie offered and loped forward to set the tin upright in the dirt, then ran the distance back and took careful aim again.

"Who?" Alerted to the name she'd never before heard, Meagan stared at Christa who glared at Livvie.

"A dance-hall lady. But Uncle Clay doesn't like her, Livvie. Not really."

"Shows what you know. I saw them talking in the street earlier."

Meagan absorbed the information. Clay was involved with

a dance-hall girl? A twinge of jealousy made her frown. Was she pretty? Is that what kept him from keeping company with her and reading to her—a woman named Beulah?

Eyes downcast, Meagan studied her hands. That morning, Penny had taken the bandages off for good. No longer a pretty ivory, the skin was blotched pink in places and shiny in others. She wondered if the dance-hall girl—Beulah—had pretty ivory hands. . . .

"Here he comes now!"

At Livvie's announcement, Meagan's head shot up, and Christa jumped to her feet. Meagan hid her hands between her knees, in the folds of her skirts. Their eyes met, and he slowed his steps, placing one boot atop the boardwalk but not coming any farther.

"Hi, Uncle Clay!" Christa threw her arms around him. "Where you been?"

"Just taking care of some business. Your ma said to tell you she needs you and Livvie both. She's at the dry-goods store, trading her pouches for supplies."

Livvie abandoned the battered tin, and she and Christa took off running down the street.

Clay seemed ill at ease. He looked Meagan's way, and she wondered if it was only business that occupied him all this time. "Good morning." His thumb and finger on the brim, he tipped his hat.

"Morning." She nodded, partly fuming, partly overjoyed to see him. She hoped he might stay and share her company.

He hesitated, then moved to the chair Penny had scooted close to Meagan's and lifted the Holy Book left there before taking a seat. The closest Meagan had been to him in days. No part of her touched him, but this near, she felt his warmth and smelled his pleasant musky scent. Her heart rate took up a faster pace with strong, unsteady beats.

"Penny been reading to you?"

" 'Til I learn how."

"That's good to know." Slumped over with his elbows on his thighs, he held the large book in his hands. His mind seemed elsewhere.

She took a chance.

"I've missed your reading to me. You have such a strong voice, so easy to hear when there's a lot of ruckus going on. And with the way you say some of those long words—you sound like a well-learned teacher."

He turned his head to look at her and grinned. "Is that right?"

She chided her breathing to remain steady. "There's so much about you that sets you apart from other men. You and your brother both have deep voices, but you. . ." She paused, wondering if she'd revealed too much.

"Go on. You've got me interested to hear what comes next."

She would *not* tell him how the sudden sound of his voice gave her delightful chills and set her blood stirring. She struggled for how to finish. "At times you talk like any other man of the West, using slang so common hereabouts. But you also sound well educated, sometimes using words beyond my grasp. So unlike your brother."

He nodded thoughtfully, shifting his focus back to the book he held. "I had the experience of my mother's training far longer than Derek. After our pa left us, my brother had to do most of the chores and didn't have time for books. But I tended to enjoy them far more than Derek ever did." He paused, his lips turning up at the corners, as if reliving those times. She admired his features, all the more attractive when he smiled. "Even when Ma got worse, she still found enough strength to see to my education. She stressed it was just as important to train the mind as it was the hands. She wanted more for me than what had become Derek's lot."

"You still miss her, don't you?"

"Every day."

"I understand."

A quiet moment elapsed as he looked at her, and a sympathetic understanding passed between them.

"The ache never really goes away, though it eases a good deal," he reassured.

"I'm glad to hear that."

He shifted in his chair. "Meagan, there's something I need to tell you."

She waited for him to go on.

"It's about Landon McClinton. He's dead."

❧

Clay watched in concern as the rosy wash of color faded from her cheeks. He'd spoken quietly, but perhaps he should have broached the subject less quickly.

Meagan pulled one hand from between her knees and pressed her palm against her bosom. "My stepfather's dead?"

"I got the telegram from Carson City this morning. Details are sketchy, but he appeared to die of heart failure during a barroom fight with his rival."

"He must have found his old partner. He went there to try to get back what the man stole from him years ago." She looked away and shook her head, dropping her hand to her skirts. "We never did get along, but I never suspected. . ."

Clay gave in to the temptation to lay his hand over hers in comfort. She jerked a bit in surprise, but didn't remove it from beneath his.

Since they'd returned to Silverton, he'd taken Penny's advice and avoided Meagan—physically. Her presence in his heart and mind, however, remained constant. After confiding to Beulah his feelings for Meagan, which had become more intense than the infatuation he'd first felt for Penny, he'd learned a portion of Beulah's history; now he further questioned his resolve to avoid Meagan. Beulah had run away, going west, after she learned the young man she loved had been killed in one of the final battles during the War Between the States. They had agreed to wait, months before the war started, since he'd had no more to give her than his heart, and a bayonet's deadly point had robbed him of even that.

Beulah urged Clay not to make the same mistake—that if he loved Meagan and knew their being together was right, to act on that love and ask her to be his wife. "Life is too fragile," she'd said. "None of us knows how much time we have left. If Will had not been so pigheaded, I would have insisted we marry no matter how poor he was. His heart was all I wanted, and if Meagan loves you like you've come to love her, I have a feeling she'll tell you the same."

Clay knew if he would yield and not cling to the Burke pride, he did have a home to offer her at Derek's up-and-coming ranch, though he doubted he could ever consider it his own or become his brother's business partner. He thought of Meagan's stepfather, so full of hatred that he'd tracked down his thieving former associate, and to what end? His own. Clay had moved past loathing his brother but still felt unable to trust Derek and questioned if he ever would be ready to take that step of good faith.

"What will you do now?" He removed his hand from Meagan's and placed it around the edge of the book.

Her hand went to join the other between her knees. "Penny's asked me to stay with her while. . ." She hesitated, clearly uncomfortable.

"While my brother and sister search for the legacy," he finished, glad his sister-in-law had offered her home. That eliminated one concern.

"Penny said I shouldn't speak of it," she explained with a rueful smile.

"You can always talk to me." Clay tried again, realizing how intimate those words sounded. "But she's correct. In mixed company, we need to keep quiet."

"Like I told her, I'd never tell a soul. I'd never do anything that might cause any of you the least amount of remorse for taking me in and being so kind."

"I didn't think you would." Clay smiled. "So, are you planning to take her up on her offer?"

"I imagine I will. I haven't anywhere else to go, and I do get along with Penny and her family, though I don't know her husband—your brother—that well."

"Don't feel bad. Neither do I." Clay's chuckle came wryly.

"But I thought you two were getting along so much better." He looked at her sharply and she shrugged. "It wasn't difficult to tell there's been trouble between you."

Clay had made no mystery of his bitterness but felt ashamed she had witnessed his failings. "It's been a long time since we've seen one another. Coming to Silverton was an unwanted reunion my pa planned for us. Matters are still shaky, but Derek and I have reached an understanding."

"I'm glad. Family can be difficult at times, but it's nice to have them around."

Clay's heart went out to her as he recalled her reason for being there.

"Tell me about your family. What was it like growing up for you?"

Clay considered her question. "As boys, Derek and I were good pals, despite the age difference. We fought hard but stayed loyal. Then one rainy morning, our pa left, having heard about a silver strike in the West. . . ."

He told her everything, sparing himself no excuse for his ill behavior toward his brother these eight years past. When he finished, she looked at him with eyes glistening in sympathy and understanding, surprising him.

"It must have been hard, you being so young and feeling all alone like that. The woman who took care of you sounds more like a jailer."

"She did treat me as her slave," Clay agreed. "But I didn't stay long."

"I'm so grateful I had you and your family to turn to after. . . what happened. I think Penny is right and God must have had a hand in us meeting."

"Now that's just what I like to see and hear," a man suddenly exclaimed from the street.

Shocked at the intrusion, Clay and Meagan turned their attention his way. A silver-haired stranger wearing a week's worth of whiskers and dusty, sweat-stained clothing approached with a toothy grin, leading his mule by a rope. He came to a halt before the hitching post. "A man holding the Lord's Book in his hands and a woman giving the Almighty the glory for her life."

"And you are?" Clay inquired.

"Preacher Dan is what the folks 'round these parts call me." He removed his battered hat, nodding to Meagan, then held out his hand to Clay. Clay reached across the hitching post and shook it. The stranger looked at Meagan. "Excuse my sorry condition, ma'am. I just returned from weeks' worth of visiting miners on their claims and haven't had opportunity to visit the bathhouse yet. Was told by the agent at the claims office that someone at the hotel needed to discuss something with me, so I wandered here first. You wouldn't by chance know Derek Burke?"

"He's my brother," Clay said with some surprise and peered more closely at the preacher's face. "Aren't you the same man who married Derek to my sister-in-law, Penny?"

"Hard to recognize under all this filth, aren't I?" Preacher Dan chuckled. "I thought you looked familiar. I had to leave in a rapid-fire hurry last time and wasn't able to talk after the wedding. I've been sworn to secrecy, a matter I've since questioned and never felt comfortable with. Giving me reason to believe I should have stayed, at least long enough to put your minds at ease."

"Pardon?" Clay tried to follow the odd man's ramblings.

Preacher Dan looked around to make sure no one stood nearby, then glanced at Meagan and back to Clay, the question apparent in his eyes.

"It's all right to speak with Miss Foster present."

"A little matter about a claim," the preacher said in a much lower tone. "And a legacy left to you and your siblings."

Clay opened his eyes wide in shock. "You know about that?"

"Sure do. I was with your pa when he drew up the map, and I gave him what little aid and guidance I could near the end, may the good Lord rest his soul."

"You knew my pa?" Clay reaffirmed, not sure he'd heard right, still stunned.

"I met him a year back when he was strong and able and as stubborn as a mule in full harness. He wanted nothing to do with me then." The preacher chuckled as if in recollection then grew sober. "After the disease struck his body, I visited him often. His mind wandered near the end; I was with him then, too. He didn't die alone."

Clay wasn't sure why he should care one whit about anything having to do with his pa, but the preacher's words oddly brought comfort.

"My brother is out at the moment," he said. "Would you mind returning later? We can talk then."

"That'll give me plenty of time to make myself presentable,"

Preacher Dan agreed. "Good day to you both." He pulled his mule around, heading in the direction of the bathhouse.

Clay watched the preacher amble down the road, sensing that, with the arrival of the lone newcomer, something significant was about to occur that would change all their lives.

❧

Meagan excused herself from the kitchen, where the Burke clan gathered around the outgoing preacher, choosing instead to be with the girls. She preferred to dwell in the fresh air and sunshine, having been cooped up amid canvas walls far too long during her convalescence. Nor did she feel comfortable being party to what clearly was a family issue.

Outside, Meagan breathed in deeply of the warm breeze. It felt good to feel her hair stir and experience the wind upon her face.

"Miss Meagan?"

She directed her attention to Christa and smiled in question.

"What do you think of the name Thunder for Uncle Clay's horse?"

"And Lightning for Pa's?" Livvie added. "Bein' as the two go together—and Pa and Uncle Clay are brothers. And bein' as they can be loud and fight—and lightning and thunder do that, too."

"Do lightning and thunder fight, Livvie?" Christa wanted to know.

"Well, they sound like it," Livvie defended. "Lightning strikes out, and thunder bellows back. And both names are strong—like Pa and Uncle Clay. They're not sissified names, like Princess Rose or Whisper."

Christa pouted. "Names aren't sissified!"

"Shows what you know." Livvie rolled her eyes skyward.

"You're mean, Livvie."

"Well, you're stupid."

"You two shouldn't always bicker," Meagan admonished softly, recalling how she and Wayne had done the same. "Be glad for these times together. They don't always last."

The two didn't respond but didn't continue squabbling, either.

Christa looked toward the street, her eyes suddenly going big. "There's Tricks!" she exclaimed, pointing to a big yellow dog.

"Tricks?" Meagan asked.

"Jinx's dog that went missing a few weeks back. I gotta tell Jinx!"

"He ain't inside the hotel." Livvie stopped Christa in her tracks. "I saw him go inside the gambling house, and you know we can't step foot near there. Besides, Mama said to stay near the hotel."

"But Tricks might run away again! And this sure wouldn't be the first time you didn't mind, Livvie."

As if the dog heard its name and didn't want to be caught, he scampered off down the road.

"Oh, no!"

Before Meagan could stop her, Christa took off running after the hound. An oath unfit for a child shot from Livvie's mouth, and she raced after her sister.

Shocked and exasperated, Meagan stared after their retreating forms, growing smaller every second, then at the hotel doorway. Should she should tell Penny the girls had run off, and with night approaching yet? She didn't want to disrupt an important meeting when she felt sure she could handle such a small matter.

Stepping off the boardwalk, she hurried after the girls.

❧

Clay sat forward on the bench, elbows on the table, and eyed the preacher who sat directly across from him. "Claim squatting?"

Preacher Dan chuckled. "A little joke on my part. Only want to reassure you folks that there's no chance of claim jumpers taking over your mine." He kept his voice down as they all did, though the preacher and the Burkes were the sole occupants of the kitchen. Most of the guests staying at the hotel were out visiting the gaming houses, dance halls, or saloons. "The claim squatters are my two nephews. Both boys have done some hard-rock mining and jumped at the chance to settle down awhile, since Bart's wife is expecting soon. I couldn't protect the area like your pa asked. My vocation won't allow it what with all the traveling I do. But you couldn't ask for better men guarding the place. Jake and Bart aren't the type to steal your claim, either—both are God-fearing, honest men."

"So there really is a mine," Derek wondered aloud, echoing Clay's thoughts.

"Almost. You'll have to bring in the machinery and man-power needed to drill."

Clay stared. "How are we supposed to gain enough capital for that? I barely have two cents to rub together and have no experience in mining."

"Neither do I," Derek agreed.

"I suggest you unearth as much ore as you can load in a wagon, enough to bring a substantial price and assure you a bank loan for the needed equipment. My nephews will help and show what needs doing. They'd jump at the chance to enter a profitable venture like this one. And both have mouths tight as beaver traps. They can keep a secret till you're ready to go public with the discovery."

"You're sure it's so profitable?" Derek asked. "I've heard stories from miners of what they hoped would be a strike that turned into little or nothing." ·

"Seen it with my own two eyes. High on a hill, a pretty vein of silver three feet wide, going straight down. No telling how far. If Michael had dug a little to the north or south, he'd of missed it. He's had it tested by an assayer. It's galena—a mixture of silver and lead—and worth a small fortune by the ton. That's a cube no more'n two and a half feet on a side. And who's to say there might not be other veins? Since your pa discovered the strike, per the regulations for ownin' claims, he gets another three hundred feet. That means he owns six hundred feet of that hill—now all yours."

They all stared at him in shock, and he grinned.

"Where'd you think I visited your pa? At a church meeting? I often ride over the land to visit with miners on their claims and see to their needs, spiritual and otherwise."

"Can you take us there?" Linda asked.

"I wish I could, little lady, but that'd go against your pa's wishes."

Kurt placed his hand on her back in comfort. Derek grunted in frustration at the man's staunch declaration, and Clay knew just how he felt.

"I may have broken my vow of silence and admitted my involvement in the matter," Preacher Dan explained, "but I didn't feel it right he should leave you to do so much worrying."

"Yeah, well, you didn't know our pa like we did," Clay grumbled. "He derived pleasure out of seeing others suffer."

"Is that a fact?" The preacher's drawl came thoughtfully, his eyes seeming to look through Clay, making him want to squirm. "Well now, I just wanted to set your minds at ease."

"I have a question," Linda said.

The preacher nodded for her to go ahead.

"Why didn't he want us to know of your involvement? We thought the clerk was the only man to know of our legacy. Whyever would our pa swear you to such secrecy?"

Preacher Dan sighed. "Sorry, ma'am, but as much as Michael

revealed to me, I couldn't begin to understand the workings of his mind. He had his reasons though. Now if you'll excuse me, I need some sleep. We can talk more in the morning if you'd like." He halted. "Oh—almost forgot. Comes with age." He grinned, pulling something from his pocket, and handed it to Derek. "Your pa did tell me to give you this."

Derek took the chain, from which a brass key dangled. "What's it for?"

"All part of the mystery." Preacher Dan winked. "You'll know soon enough."

Once he left, they stared at the key and questioned what it led to. Hearing a step outside, they quieted, and Derek pocketed the key.

Shorty rushed past the curtain. His excited gaze latched onto Kurt.

"Amos and Jonesy Greer are in town!"

Kurt jumped up from the bench, reaching for his rifle. "Where?"

"Dunno. Just heard from Tucker and came to tell you. They told him to spread the news they're looking for Derek Burke." Shorty glanced at Derek with something akin to awe that the outlaws would ask for him by name.

Penny clutched her husband's arm, shock written on her face. Derek remained dead calm, though his eyes snapped with disgust and anger.

"Those are the boys who shot Marshal Wilson and robbed the gold shipment a few months back," Kurt said. "They probably think they're safe from getting caught with no lawman in town. They've got another thing coming." He kissed his wife's cheek, warning her to stay in the hotel with the others and keep her derringer close.

"I'll take you to Tucker." Shorty hurried after Kurt.

Penny suddenly jumped up from the table. "Wait—the

girls! Were they sitting on the hotel boardwalk like I told them to?"

"No, ma'am. Didn't see no one outside." Shorty moved away from the curtain.

Derek grabbed his wife's arm before she could follow. "Let me handle this. You have the baby to consider."

"I canna just stay and do nothing! The girls could be in trouble."

"I'll see to it." His firm tone brooked no refusal. "Stay here. I mean it, Penny. I don't want you anywhere near those scoundrels again."

Clay rose, his grave stare meeting Derek's. "I'll help." His heart beat hard against his ribs in dread when he remembered Meagan had gone with the girls.

His brother hesitated. "You got a gun?"

"Pa's old shotgun."

Derek winced and handed him one of his pistols. "Know how to fire one of these?"

Clay nodded and took the weapon.

Linda slipped her arm around Penny's shoulders. "It'll be all right. We'll pray and ask God to keep the girls safe. Likely they only took off wandering as they often do and are just fine."

Before he left with Derek, Clay heard the tremor in his sister's voice and realized she didn't believe a word she said.

twelve

Meagan lost sight of the girls and went on intuition alone. Without her forming it, a prayer drifted to her mind. *Please God, help me find them before they get in more trouble.*

She ignored the outright stares she received from a number of men, most of them near the saloons, and hurried through the street, peering between buildings. Hearing a dog bark up ahead, then give a sharp yelp, she picked up her skirts and raced toward the sound. She turned the corner near the livery and stopped dead in her tracks. The yellow dog ran past her.

Christa stood, trapped by a burly man who stealthily approached. Her eyes wide with fright, she backed up until her backside hit the wall.

"Well, if it ain't the little Injun gal," the stranger said, his tone chillingly familiar. "Your pa wouldn't be Derek Burke, now, would he?"

Christa began to cry.

"Shut up. I know who you are and what your pa has. And I want it."

Meagan stepped forward, ready to attack and beat the rogue with her fists. He moved to snatch up Christa, and she glimpsed his profile. She froze in stunned terror, then slipped back around the corner of the building, pressing her shoulders to the wall. Her heart pounded so hard and painful, she thought she might die as unwanted memories gripped her: held in his ruthless grasp; the reviling way he took liberties; his taunts as he almost drowned her, tried to have his way with her—he and his brother murdering her family.

Now he had Christa.

The reminder that there were two made her scan the area, panicked, but she didn't see his brother or anyone else for that matter. She must help Christa—didn't dare run off out of fear or to secure help. She'd done that once. She would not fail a second time.

"Get your hands off my sister!"

Meagan's blood froze when she heard Livvie's order. She peeked around the corner. The girl must have been hidden before.

"Livvie!" Christa cried before the man's huge hand covered her mouth.

"You want her back?" he asked Livvie, facing Meagan's direction. "You tell your pa to meet me and my brother here in a quarter of an hour. Or your little sister is as good as dead."

Christa's frightened cry came like a weak kitten's mew behind his hand.

Livvie glared at him, her legs apart, arms akimbo as if she might run up and punch him in the stomach or kick his shins.

No, Meagan silently pleaded. *Livvie, you don't know who you're dealing with. God, please help them escape. Help me do what I can.*

The evil stranger turned and walked away with Christa. Before Meagan could act, Livvie raced after him.

"I know what you want! And I know where it is, too."

In the falling twilight, Meagan's gaze fell on a pitchfork leaning against the opposite building. To get to it, she would have to step out where he could see her, which could endanger Christa further. Or the scoundrel might let the child loose and grab Meagan to finish what he and his brother started weeks ago.

The horrific thought made her insides churn, but she couldn't let him further harm the children. She must be patient and strong, must wait for an opportune moment. *God help me. I'm terrified. Give me the courage I need so badly.*

The outlaw turned to face Livvie. "What does a little Injun runt like you know?"

"I know there's a mine—Pa's mine. And you're wanting the map that leads to it." He started in surprise, and she nodded. "I know where Pa hid it. Let my sister go, and I'll take you there."

"How about you take me there this second, or I break her scrawny neck like a twig?"

Christa squealed in panicked fear as he jerked her head sideways with his hand. Tears ran down her cheeks.

"Okay!" Livvie yelled. "Just don't hurt her."

"Take me there now."

"Okay," Livvie said, subdued. "It's over there."

He looked to where she pointed. "Behind the livery? You expect me to believe your pa hid the map in a public place?" He did something to make Christa squeal beneath his palm. "Think again."

"He did! Honest! He hid it in the eaves. Didn't want to keep it on him for fear someone might take it when he was sleeping." She tentatively walked his way and moved ahead. "I'll show you."

The two moved out of sight, and Meagan darted across the area, grabbing the pitchfork. Her fingers ached holding the iron handle, hot from being in the sun all day. But she didn't release her grip. Silently, she followed until they came into view and halted, waiting for the right moment to attack.

"Aye." Livvie pointed up. "More to the left, near them yellow flowers."

He stopped and looked at her in suspicion. "You get it."

"I would, but I can't reach."

While he stared at the eaves, Livvie made eye contact with Christa. A signal seemed to pass between them. Livvie slowly backed up, pulled her slingshot from the twine at her waist and bent to retrieve a small rock. She positioned it in the sling, her hands down in the folds of her dress, and slowly lifted the weapon to eye level.

"Now, Christa!"

"Ah!" The rogue released Christa and shook his hand in pain. "You little brat, you bit me!" She fell to the dirt, jumped up, and sped toward Livvie, who let her missile fly. It made a dull *thwunk* in the eaves above the outlaw's head. Meagan stepped into sight, motioning to Christa, as a dark buzzing cloud descended on the villain.

"Oww!" he yelped in pain. Foul curses flew from his mouth as he slapped at the cloud of bees, then dunked his head and shoulders in a nearby trough of stagnant water, drowning most of the poor winged bugs.

"Run back to the hotel, Christa. Don't stop for anyone," Meagan whispered when the child raced to her and threw her trembling arms around her skirts. Meagan patted her hair. "Hurry now. Tell your pa and uncles what happened. You, too, Livvie—run!"

The girls nodded and sped away. Realizing his prey was escaping, the outlaw went in pursuit and might have caught up, but Meagan stepped into sight, blocking his path, the tines of the pitchfork aimed at the vile creature's belly. Several of the bees still buzzed around, but they seemed intent on his flesh and not her own.

"We meet again," she seethed between her teeth, glaring at him. "Only this time I'm not running away."

❧

"Pa!"

Clay and Derek swung around upon hearing Christa scream. Derek opened his arms to his youngest, who flew into them, wrapping her arms tightly around his neck.

"The bad men on the trail are in town," Livvie said breathlessly. "One of 'em got Christa."

Horror swept across Derek's face as he gently unearthed Christa's face from where she'd buried it in his shoulder. "You all right, sweetheart?"

She nodded, tears shining in her big dark eyes. Clay noticed the fingerlike bruises at Christa's jaw at the same time Derek did. His mouth firmed into a line, white around the edges. Clay also felt like punching whoever had done this to his little niece.

"Livvie, where's Meagan?" His blood chilled when he realized she hadn't run up behind the girls.

"She cornered the bad man with a pitchfork so we could get away. Pa—it was the same man who tried to hurt Mama."

"Where, Livvie?"

"In back of the livery. He wanted the map."

"Just one man?" Derek tried to set Christa down, but she held on tighter. "Run on back to the hotel to your mama, sweetheart."

"No, please, Pa! Don't let me go," Christa begged, terrified from the ordeal she'd suffered. She held Derek's neck in a death grip, wrapping her legs more tightly around his waist and pressing herself close, as if she might crawl into him. Clearly, she needed her father.

"You take the girls back to Penny," Clay said. "I'll take care of this."

"Clay! Wait!"

He raced off before Derek could do more than call out his name.

ঙ

The villain glared back at Meagan from eyes that had begun to swell from the stings. She kept her grip firm on the pitchfork, though her hands felt as if they were again touching fire and ached something fierce.

"A snake like you deserves all the torment you get—and more besides," she hissed.

His eyes sparked, and she realized he now remembered her. "The girl by the river. Gave my brother a broken nose and me a passel of bruises."

"Say the word, and I'll gladly do it again."

His smile came sinister. "Got you a lot of pluck, gal. But I wonder if you'd act so high and mighty if you knew that your brother got down on his knees and begged me not to shoot him—right before I pulled the trigger."

His admission made her want to retch. Her body began to tremble. "Stop it."

"And your ma begged Jonesy to tell where you was, worried some calamity had befallen you. We assured her it had." He chuckled and slapped a bee buzzing near his arm, killing it with the palm of his meaty hand. "Yep, I reckon that took the smug look off your face."

"No more," she whispered. Her grip on the pitchfork loosened, and she felt as if she might collapse from the shock of hearing the horrifying details.

"She begged him not to barricade her in the shack right before I told him to set fire to it. If she'd been more hospitable, we might have let them be. But she wouldn't give us grub when we asked, and you wouldn't get us water. Your brother had the nerve to wave around a shotgun and demand we leave. So we backtracked and took him by surprise."

"You are the most evil, despicable vermin ever to walk the earth—"

From behind, someone wrenched the pitchfork from her hands at the same time a man's strong arm wound painfully around her ribs and pulled her against him. She struggled for breath.

"Hold her tight, Jonesy. She ain't getting away from us this time."

❧

Near the livery, Clay saw no one. Twilight had deepened, the shadows making the darkness thicker. A light flickered behind the livery, and he followed it.

"I'm not getting on your horse. You can't make me." Meagan's voice came clear, and Clay's heart jumped in both panic and relief.

"We could kill you," a man suggested.

"Go ahead. You've taken everything else of mine."

"Not everything. . ."

At the man's evil gibe, Clay's skin crawled. He peered around the corner.

Meagan stood with her back against a man who held her trapped. Her face shone like an angel's in the light of a lamp. Resolute. Unafraid. Calm—stunning Clay. Another man faced her.

"What do you say, Amos? Reckon we ought to tie her up and throw her over the saddle?"

"Reckon we should. We'll come back later for the map." He turned to get some rope, and Clay made his move. A few steps, and he cocked the trigger, aiming the muzzle at her captor's head.

"Let her go, or you're a dead man."

"Amos?" the man questioned, as if he didn't possess a mind of his own.

"Do it," the other man grunted.

Jonesy released her. She hurried to Clay, who grabbed her arm and pulled her close. He took a moment to glance at her, keeping the gun at the outlaw's head. "You all right?"

She nodded.

"Put your guns on the ground," Clay ordered Jonesy, "and

kick them over here." He took the brace of pistols from Jonesy's gun belt, handing them to Meagan, then picked up Amos's guns, tucking them in his pants.

"Let's get you out of here," he whispered, his hand going to her waist.

They'd only taken a few steps when a shot rang through the air and one of the men yowled in pain. Clay turned in surprise. Jonesy held his bleeding arm. A knife lay at his feet. Amos was nowhere in sight.

He looked back to the street and noticed Derek standing there, a smoking gun in his hand. "You almost had a knife in your back," he explained to Clay. "I'll take care of him till Kurt arrives. You take her back to the hotel."

Clay nodded. "Thanks."

"No need to thank me. I'll always take care of you, little brother."

Anxious to get Meagan back to safety, Clay said nothing more.

thirteen

Meagan stood outside in the cool of the evening. The only noise came from the tinny player piano inside a nearby dance hall and cheers from the men inside. Kurt had returned five minutes earlier to grimly report he had shot Amos, who'd found another gun during his attempted escape and fired at Kurt. One of the Greer brothers lay stone dead in a wagon outside; the other sat wounded in the livery, since no jailhouse existed, with a guard posted outside until Kurt returned.

Meagan wasn't sure what she felt. Relief, certainly. Unease. Sorrow.

Kurt told them Jonesy had been blubbering for his dead brother. A simple-minded man, Jonas Greer offered no resistance and needed to be told what to do at every turn. Linda wanted to despise him for setting fire to their shack at his brother's orders but couldn't help feeling a twinge of sympathy. What chance did a man like that have with a brother like Amos? And to learn that those same two had tried to attack Penny. . .

A step on the boards behind made her whirl around, still tense from her encounter with the outlaws.

Clay looked at her in apology. "Sorry to have startled you."

She smiled to see his handsome face. "I'm just glad it's over. I talked with Preacher Dan, and he helped put my mind at ease." She had told of how she appealed to God when Christa was in danger, and the preacher taught her more about Him. How the Lord had been born to a virgin, died blameless on a cross, and was resurrected. Amazed, she had listened to the most fascinating story she'd ever heard, a tale that was true, and at her agreement, he'd led her in prayer, asking Jesus to be her Savior and Lord.

"I talked to Preacher Dan, too. He helped me see areas where I've thought wrong, especially about Ma's death. For everyone, there's an appointed time to die, and sometimes, no matter how we pray, it's inevitable." Clay stepped closer to Meagan, his manner seeming both vulnerable and determined. "When I knew the Greer brothers had you, I prayed hard, harder than I've ever prayed. This time, God answered—it wasn't your appointed time—and I'm indebted to Him for life."

Something about his expression made her catch her breath. His eyes were intent, glistening with unshed tears. He took her hands in his own, looking down at them. Remembering their appearance, she pulled them away.

"Did I hurt you?" he asked in concern, looking up again.

"No, it's just. . ."

"You don't want me touching you." His words came dull, making her sorry she'd reacted.

"It's not that at all." She averted her gaze again, feeling her face warm.

"Then what?"

She shook her head, feeling petty to give in to vanity after all that had happened. "They're ugly."

At her whisper, he again took hold of her hands. His thumbs caressed hers. "No, angel."

Her heart melted at his endearment.

"They're badges of honor—the hands of a woman of strong will and courage. A woman who'd sacrifice herself for those she loves. A woman I would love to call wife." As he spoke, he lifted both her hands and kissed each in turn. His soft hair brushed her mottled skin, and she stared at his lowered head in surprise. She felt she might swoon at his sweet words and touch.

He lifted his gaze. "Surely you must know how I feel about you, Meagan?"

"But you've been so distant. . . ." She felt breathless with the manner in which he stared, his eyes shining deep blue in the lantern light.

"I had plenty of things to sort out—I didn't want to confuse you when I didn't know my own mind. I've decided to accompany my brother to search for our legacy and to become his partner at the ranch. He saved my life tonight; I can trust him. And I want you to be part of that life, too, Meagan. Before Preacher Dan leaves Silverton tomorrow, I want him to marry us if you'll have me. Say you will."

Her breath caught. "What about Beulah?"

"Beulah?" His brow creased. "How do you know about Beulah?"

"Livvie told me you were interested in her—"

"Livvie needs to learn to keep quiet when she doesn't know what she's talking about." His warm hands cupped her face. "Beulah is a friend who helped me through some rough times. It's you I love, Meagan, you I want to spend my life with."

Before she could say yes, his cool lips found hers, soon growing warm, his touch making her head spin. Happier than she could remember, she wound her fingers through his hair and, with her kiss, silently gave him her answer.

❧

In the breaking dawn, Meagan stood beside Clay, their family near, and recited her vows. Joy as golden as sunshine brimmed over inside her heart. It didn't matter that their wedding took place in a dusty street, with many of the townsmen stopping work to watch. Or that, instead of wedding bells, the sound of pickaxes rang through the air. She would become Mrs.

Clayton Burke and would now share a lifetime with the man she loved.

That was all that mattered.

Holding tightly to the pretty bouquet of wildflowers Christa had picked, Meagan smiled.

Preacher Dan pronounced them man and wife, and Clay kissed her amid Christa's squeals and Livvie's handclaps—and a few good-natured jests from Derek and Kurt. Penny and Linda gently admonished their husbands while Livvie began playing a sweet lilting tune on her harmonica and Christa skipped and danced around them.

Meagan looked into Clay's eyes, finding herself there.

"I love you so," she said quietly, so only he could hear. "I knew it for certain when you tried to read that poetry book and got so nervous. Will you read it to me, now that we're wed?"

"Whatever you desire, angel. But I plan on us making our own poetry."

He smiled in a way that made her heart race and kissed her again.

❧

Clay, Linda, and Derek searched for more than a week—and finally found the short canyon with their hill of silver, meeting the preacher's nephews who guarded it. They supped together and talked for hours, at the end of which both Jake and Bart agreed to team up with Derek and Clay to unearth the ore. It would take some time before they had enough to commence with the plan Preacher Dan suggested, and Clay was grateful to God for their successes so far, but he only wanted to get back to his new wife.

Three days and nights with Meagan had been like granting a dying man a dipperful of water, then sending him back to the desert. The memory of the feel of her in his embrace made him want to speed up the process so he could return to the haven of her soft arms. At least she was safe and comfortable with Penny and the girls in their home in the valley.

Kurt had been unable to join the search, needing to return Jonas Greer to Jasperville, where he would be tried and hanged. Though his life on the earth would soon end in punishment for his crimes, his life in the Great Beyond would just begin with a Savior who'd forgiven all of them. Preacher Dan had visited the simple man, ministering to him, and the former outlaw had tearfully repented of his multitude of sins and given his heart over to God. After Kurt told the family, Clay had held Meagan close that night, seeing her upset, but she'd told him her tears were ones of relief.

"I've seen enough death," she'd whispered against his chest. "I thought I'd be pleased to hear Amos was dead, but I don't feel the satisfaction I'd hoped for. He must have gone to an eternity of hellfire, and I can't be happy about that for any man. Jonesy will receive his just punishment—yet at least his suffering will be brief, not eternal." She moved to look at him, pressing her hand against his jaw. "But I don't want to think about any of that right now. I just want to think about us and the wonderful life we'll have together."

Clay had stared at her, amazed. "You're incredible," he'd whispered, then kissed her soft, warm lips. "So beautiful. . ." His mouth had traveled to her slender neck and along the perfect slope of her shoulder. . . .

"We were told to give you this," Jake's gruff voice broke into Clay's pleasant memory. Grudgingly, he brought his attention back to the present and the barren land on which they now camped.

The preacher's nephews looked young, but their strapping builds would certainly deter claim jumpers. Jake set a small chest in front of the Burkes. "It was partly hidden in the scrub at the foot of the hill."

His wife, Edna, moved silently, filling their tins with coffee; then the three new members of the team disappeared inside a tent, giving the Burkes privacy.

Brothers and sister looked at one another before Derek took the chain with the key that Preacher Dan had given him from around his neck. He fitted it into the lock and turned it with ease.

"What's inside?" Linda asked.

"A Bible," Derek said in shock, lifting it and thumbing through the pages. A piece of paper fell out, and Clay grabbed it.

"Well?" Derek asked once Clay unfolded it.

"It's from our pa."

"Don't keep us in the dark," Linda urged.

" 'To my own: Derek, Clayton, Linda,' " Clay read aloud. " 'You must be wondering why I drew up a map, with orders each of you was to get a piece, then led you on this long hunt. Well, if you're reading this, you must not have killed each other by now, so I'm assuming you quit being so stubborn, boys, and learned to work together. And that you all spent a fair amount of time getting to know one another. Good. 'Cause that was my intent all along....' "

Clay stopped reading, and the three stared at each other, stunned.

"Go on," Linda urged. "What else does it say?"

" 'I did wrong by each of you, and your mothers, and I'm powerful sorry. I was an ornery, selfish old cuss. My dying wish is that you won't let what heartache I sowed ruin your becoming a family. That and this book are the best treasures I could wish for you, something I learned too late for one but not the other. Oh, you get the silver, too, and I want Preacher Dan to have a share for all he's done and for writing this here letter since I never learned how (side note from Preacher Dan: The share isn't necessary).' "

Derek chuckled and Clay smiled. "Sounds like something he would say."

"But he will have his share," Linda affirmed.

"Absolutely," both brothers responded at once.

Clay went on reading. " 'Derek—you've been a good boy, helping your ma when I wasn't around, becoming man of the family before you were old enough for whiskers. I'm proud of you, son. But don't let your yearning for adventure and riches cloud your judgment like I did. You're more like me than you realize; I want better for you than that.' "

Clearly moved, Derek ducked his head, pulling his hat low.

" 'Clayton—I hope you're still reading them books, son. I gave you a hard time about it when you should have been doing chores, but truth is, I admired you for your brains and wished I'd learned how. Maybe then I could have written my own blasted letter.' " Clay whisked his fingers over his damp lashes so he could see to read the rest.

" 'Linda—I wish we'd met. I heard about your ma's recent passing and wish I could have helped somehow, but I hear you're as beautiful and strong-willed as ever she was, so you'll do all right. Boys—I'm picturing the look on your saintly mother's face and have to chuckle, hoping she won't flat keel over when she sees me approach the pearly gates. To think a wandering preacher finally got through my thick skull; if it weren't for this disease, I might have never listened. So I both curse and bless what's become my lot.' "

They stared at each other in shock, not knowing what to say.

"Pa found God?" Derek shook his head in wonder. "I would have never believed it possible."

Neither would Clay. He read on: " 'You children might not understand, but I did love both your mothers after my own fashion, as well as I knew how. Soon I'll join them, that is, if they don't kick me out once they see me. I imagine I'll get quite an earful from both. I only wanted to strike it rich for all of us, take your ma back East and find her a good doctor, boys—and Linda, I don't regret one hour of knowing your ma since the day I stumbled through her town, dyin' of thirst, and she fetched me water from the well—but it was in her best interest I left. If I'd known what troubles she would face afterward with them snobs she came west with, if I'd known you existed, little Linda, I would have done what I could to help. I learned too late. My greed and wrong ways of thinking and doing cost me my family and my health, something I deeply regret. I looked for silver and found it but won't live to enjoy the reward of my labors. You do that for me, but don't let the stubborn Burke blood that also runs through your veins come between you and God or family, you hear?'"

"We won't, Pa," Linda whispered.

"There's more," Clay said. " 'Linda, find a good, trustworthy man for a husband, one who'll stay by your side and you can depend on.'"

"I have." She laughed through her tears.

" 'Derek, Clayton—a good woman is more precious than rubies, at least that's what this Good Book Preacher Dan read to me says. I reckon she's more precious than silver, too.'" Clay thought about Meagan and smiled wistfully. " 'Find a wife who's honest and true and will stick with you through bad times. Enjoy the wealth, enjoy each other, but remember, the three of you: What this chest contains is the most satisfying treasure you could ever own. Sincerely, and with much remorse and regret, I am your erstwhile pa, Michael Aloysius Burke,'" Clay finished and lay the letter down.

Silence thickened the air as each of them stared at the paper, then at each other.

"He may not have given us much when he was alive," Derek said at last. "But he did bring us together."

"To be a family," Linda added, holding her hand out to Derek, who took it. "Never again in want." She held her other hand out to Clay. He took it, then reached for Derek's hand. The three sat, hands clasped, and grinned at one another.

"And for all that, Pa, we're eternally grateful," Clay finished for all of them.

epilogue

Three years later

Meagan nursed her tiny daughter, Eloise, as she sat with Linda and Penny on the veranda of their sprawling ranch house. The women kept a watchful eye on the children who frolicked near the stream. Yellow and blue butterflies flitted around, the spring evening pleasantly warm as the women lazed in the shade.

Livvie piggybacked her little sister, Kimama, whom they called Kim for short. Christa helped her brother, Angus Aloysius, named for both Penny's Scots grandda and Derek's pa, to take small steps. Holding his chubby hands, she jumped up and down after each accomplishment made, almost knocking the tot over.

"Careful, Christa," Penny admonished. "And do watch out for Wayne! You don't want to knock your cousin into the water."

Meagan shook her head and smiled, noting her two-year-old digging his fingers into the moist streambed—likely to find worms. "Christa," she called. "Make sure Wayne isn't eating what he finds."

"I will, Aunt Meagan," the girl promised. Her frightful experience with the outlaws hadn't altered her sweet nature; the most visible change she'd undergone, the height to her slender frame. Now she stood mere inches shorter than Livvie.

Since their ordeal in Silverton, Livvie had grown far more tolerant of Christa and, at fourteen, was blossoming into a young woman. Meagan noticed her attention often drifted

166

to a tall, strapping ranch hand who'd just turned sixteen. Still, Meagan wondered if the day would really ever arrive when Livvie would trade in her long braids and slingshot for pinned-up hair and longer skirts.

Eloise pulled away and cooed. Meagan adjusted her blouse, smiling down into her daughter's beautiful blue eyes.

"She has Clay's eyes, too," Penny murmured.

"I know, and I love that. Though Clay told me he'd like it if our next child has golden eyes and hair like mine." He often complimented both in words as lovely as any poet's, making her blush.

Penny laughed. "Did he now?"

"I miss him. They've been gone for weeks."

"I know. I miss Derek, too. At least we women have each other while our men are away on business."

Meagan covered Penny's hand with her own. "And I'm so grateful for that."

Clay kept accounts for the ranch and mine but often rode with Derek on visits to oversee the mine's production and on cattle drives, like now. They'd hired managers and workers for each, but the Burke brothers preferred getting their own hands dirty. They ran their ranch because they enjoyed hard work, not because they needed income. Owning tens of millions may have altered their circumstances, but it hadn't jaded their characters. Meagan rejoiced to see how unaffected they were by their wealth and how their bond of brotherhood and friendship had prospered.

But oh, how she missed her husband!

After three full years of marriage and two children, their love had only grown deeper. Sometimes, he cradled her in his arms and read to her from Browning, and they softly laughed about the first time he'd tried to read from the same book. She loved to hear his rich voice recite the beautiful words, though she could now read. And write. Her hands were scarred, but she'd regained full use of them. And she'd written her daydreams into collections of short stories he'd urged her to publish. But they were private, the wanderings of her heart. Maybe someday in the future she would gain courage and share them with the world. . . .

"The men should be returning soon," Linda said, breaking into Meagan's thoughts. "They're never gone longer than three weeks at a time." She cradled her five-month-old little girl, Faith, an answer to her fervent prayers. After two years of marriage, Linda feared she might be barren when month after month brought no child inside her belly. Faith proved it wasn't so, and the slight bulge beneath Linda's skirts attested that Faith might have a brother or sister come autumn.

"As much as you're with us, you really should have built your home closer than just outside Silverton," Meagan teased.

Linda laughed. "We would have, but Kurt has to watch over things there, though he enjoys going on these drives when he gets the chance. Shorty has done well as deputy, and Kurt feels confident leaving him in charge." With his success in ending the notorious Greer brothers' reign of terror, the people of Silverton begged Kurt to stay on as sheriff, even building a jailhouse. An encouraging telegram from his mentor aided his decision.

"And Beulah? How is she?"

"I'm still trying to encourage her to leave her life at the dance hall." Linda deeply sympathized with Beulah's situation since hers had once been similar. "She's expressed a desire to go back East to her family, so I'm hopeful. They never approved of the boy she loved, and when he was killed at Appomattox, she was hurt and angered by their indifference and came west. Since Preacher Dan spoke with her, I think she's ready to put that bitterness behind her now. I told her I'd do all I can to help, of course—buy her a train ticket, suitable clothes, whatever she needs. But you know how she is." Linda shook her head. "Please continue praying for her."

"I will," Meagan reassured. "Clay and I do every morning." Beulah possessed a compassionate heart and had wished Meagan well after her marriage to Clay, sincerely happy for them both. It didn't take Meagan long to see why Clay considered her a friend. In their concern for her, Clay and Linda had each offered the vivacious redhead money to start a new life, but Beulah wouldn't take it.

Profits from the mine had made the Burkes and their associates wealthy overnight. For himself, the preacher took only a small portion of his share, which the Burkes had needed to force upon him, and gave the rest to charities. Kurt and Linda sent a tidy sum to his aunt Doreen in Jasperville, to help fulfill her dreams of funding a charity for poor miners and their families and for building a church. The Burkes also gave, and eight months earlier, they hit the mother lode, a bonanza that had all the state buzzing and brought mine workers out in droves. A mining town had sprung up—Prosperity—and Clay and Derek had built a home there, too. But all the Burkes preferred the peaceful, open spaces of their beautiful B & B Ranch.

Meagan had never owned so many gowns, all of them fine, or seen so many jewels as Clay gifted her with, the last a ruby pendant. Each time he presented her with a necklace or earbobs or a bracelet, she quietly protested, telling him all she needed was his love, and each time he smiled and told her she would always have that, but it pleased him to give her the world if he could since she was so precious to him. Soon she hoped to give him a gift, one she'd toiled over for days. . . .

"They're here!" Livvie shouted, running down the wildflower-laden hill where she'd wandered. "I just saw them over the rise."

Her heart drumming madly with anticipation, Meagan laid Eloise in her carved cradle and glanced at the east wing of their sprawling ranch house, where she and Clay resided. Tonight, he would be there with her, his strong arms holding her. She missed his loving and their long, intimate talks late into the night. Even with their two children and nurse sharing the same wing, Meagan felt lonely without her husband near.

"With dinnertime upon us, I suppose I should be lettin' François know," Penny muttered, though her eyes were alight with excitement. "If I hurry, I can return before they ride over the hill." She winked at Meagan, who laughed. Though they had servants, Penny often preferred to do her own cooking, to the chef's displeasure—a Frenchman Clay hired two years before who, much to everyone's amusement, crossed opinions with Penny whenever she entered his kitchen.

"There they are!" Christa squealed, grabbing up her little brother. She ran with Livvie to meet the men approaching on horseback. The children's nurses came outdoors to collect their small charges, and Penny abandoned her errand.

The three women rushed to greet their returning husbands.

Clay dismounted and swung Meagan around, then kissed her hard. She held onto him as if she might never let go.

"I missed you, angel," he murmured against her hair. "You're all I thought of."

"I'm so thankful to God that you're home and safe."

After another kiss, this one long and gentle, they walked arm in arm to the ranch house behind Derek and Penny, and Kurt and Linda. A stable hand rushed to take the horses.

"How are the children?" Clay asked, handing over the reins.

"Eloise can lift her head now."

"Can she?" He chuckled.

"And Wayne still enjoys his daily mud baths."

He let out a deep belly laugh, squeezing her close to his

side. "That's my boy!"

Meagan smiled. "Lightning foaled. Christa named the colt Little Cloud."

"Interesting name."

"And I have a surprise for you."

He abruptly stopped walking and swung around to look in her eyes, then below her waist.

She laughed. "No, not news of another child. At least not yet."

"What else would cause you such excitement?"

"First, you need a good meal to fill your belly—and a hot bath to relax. Then I'll tell you."

"Mmm. After weeks of riding in dust and wind to find good pasture, with only cattle and irritable kin missing their wives for company, that sounds like music to my ears."

She hugged him close. He did look weary but happy.

After they'd eaten and said their good nights to the family, once she'd tucked the children in bed, she dismissed the maid and personally drew Clay a steaming bath in their claw-footed tub, waiting hand and foot on him like a loving slave to her king. Afterward, he drew her close in their huge bed, which no longer felt so empty, and looked deeply into her eyes.

"Tell me your surprise."

She smiled but, now that the moment had arrived, felt nervous. "I wrote a poem. For you." Leaning over to reach the table beside their bed, she picked up a paper scroll wrapped with a red satin ribbon and handed it to him.

As he read, she softly spoke the same words that were a part of her soul:

> *"In your absence, the stars shine less brightly,*
> *My heart grows heavy, laden with storms;*
> *I yearn to pull you to me so tightly,*
> *Our lips pressed together, so warm.*

> *In your arms I am whole and complete,*
> *My universe achieves balance when*
> *Your presence so needed, so sweet,*
> *Makes me whole and alive once again.*
>
> *I pray you return to me, never to part,*
> *You are all I require, you are my very heart."*

Clay looked up from the paper, his eyes glistening.

"It's not as good as Browning," she apologized. "But it's how I feel."

"It's better than Browning." He laid the poem aside and drew her close. "It's how I feel about you, too, angel. You're my real treasure. Not the silver. Not the ranch. I've missed you so, and each time gets worse. It's been so long. . . ." His voice came hoarse. He kissed her passionately, and she melted against his strength.

"Much too long," she breathed near his mouth, "but oh, the homecomings are so sweet. . . ."

Clay showed her without further words just how much he agreed.

A Letter To Our Readers

Dear Reader:

In order that we might better contribute to your reading enjoyment, we would appreciate your taking a few minutes to respond to the following questions. We welcome your comments and read each form and letter we receive. When completed, please return to the following:

Fiction Editor
Heartsong Presents
PO Box 719
Uhrichsville, Ohio 44683

1. Did you enjoy reading *A Treasure Revealed* by Pamela Griffin?
   ❏ Very much! I would like to see more books by this author!
   ❏ Moderately. I would have enjoyed it more if

   _____

   _____

   _____

2. Are you a member of **Heartsong Presents**? ❏ Yes ❏ No
   If no, where did you purchase this book? _____

   _____

3. How would you rate, on a scale from 1 (poor) to 5 (superior), the cover design? _____

4. On a scale from 1 (poor) to 10 (superior), please rate the following elements.

   ____ Heroine   ____ Plot
   ____ Hero   ____ Inspirational theme
   ____ Setting   ____ Secondary characters

5. These characters were special because? _____
_____
_____

6. How has this book inspired your life? _____
_____
_____

7. What settings would you like to see covered in future
   Heartsong Presents books? _____
_____
_____

8. What are some inspirational themes you would like to see
   treated in future books? _____
_____
_____

9. Would you be interested in reading other **Heartsong
   Presents** titles? ❏ Yes   ❏ No

10. Please check your age range:
    ❏ Under 18   ❏ 18-24
    ❏ 25-34   ❏ 35-45
    ❏ 46-55   ❏ Over 55

Name _____
Occupation _____
Address _____
City, State, Zip _____